The Reluctant Assassin

by

Bip Wetherell

Chapter One

The First Assassination

12 October 1917. Ypres Salient, Belgium

Captain Mark Stevens was 21 years old, 6 feet 2 inches and weighed 12 stone. As he sat in the shell hole that passed for a trench waiting to go over the top on the first day of the Battle of Passchendaele, you could see no fear in his blue eyes. A man used to the horrors and degradation of the First World War, there was just a look of grim determination to get the job done. He looked at his watch to ensure he blew his whistle to signal his men into battle at the synchronised time of 6am. Five thousand French, Canadian, English and German men would die that day. A mixture of. Today was not the day for Mark Stevens to kill any Germans though. He had been given a specific job to do. He had been sent there to assassinate an English officer.

****

The Military Club, London, England

Established in 1630 for the purpose of providing superb accommodation, good food and wine, the service at the Military Club was renowned. Officers of all rank, regardless of which regiment they belonged to, could join this exclusive club as long as they could provide two things: a first class sponsor who would stand for them at the induction interview, and secondly, a healthy bank balance that could provide the 10 guineas fee to join.

As well as the restaurant and the well-stocked bar, the club provided 25 bedrooms to be used if the men needed to stay in London overnight or for a couple of days. There was a small rear entrance that was used for deliveries of stock, etc. and also young ladies when it was deemed appropriate. Just inside the rear entrance up a separate stairway, there was a dining room that was only used for small, private, gatherings. On the last Sunday evening of every month, a small band of politicians, all ex-soldiers, had exclusive use of the room. The food was laid out in a buffet style, and the wine was already uncorked and placed into ice buckets, so there was no need for staff to attend. After the fourth politician arrived, the door was locked.

"Has No 7 arrived in France yet?" The senior man at the head of the table was in his seventies but was obviously the man in charge.

The youngest of the four, the newcomer, replied, "He arrived three weeks ago and has been given a platoon of the King's Own Riflemen under his command as captain."

The second of the men, who was there to write down the minutes of the meeting, went to speak but was interrupted by the third man.

"We know we cannot give the Directive for the kill without No 7's final authority, but it is a nightmare over there. Communications are sporadic, and No 7 has missed his last two meetings with his radio operator as the front line has not been relieved for the last seven days. For all we know, he could be dead by now."

The Directive had been formed only that year to deal with situations that could never be dealt with in the correct manner if it was decided to go through the normal channels. Only one man had been selected and had been highly trained for special assignments. After the man had been sworn in, he had been given his own number and was never referred to by his real name. The very existence of such a trained operative was only known by the four men in the room and one other, His Majesty the King.

There was silence in the room whilst all four men contemplated the situation. It was the law of the Directive that once a target had been discussed, and the kill was approved, the man who had to carry out the task had the right to ensure that the decision was the correct one. All they could do was wait.

When Captain Mark Stevens arrived in France, his first job was to contact the commanding officer of the King's Own Riflemen to explain his posting. It took him two days to finally track down the regiment's headquarters in an old disused farmhouse a couple of miles behind the lines near the village of Passchendaele.

Brigadier Gwyn Evans was a soldier of the old school and showed disgust when Stevens reported that he had been sent to trace an officer suspected of relaying information to the enemy. When Mark explained that he wanted to serve alongside the suspect in the front line, Evans stated his confusion.

"Why can't we just haul the beggar out, court-martial him, and have him shot at dawn?"

"Insufficient evidence," replied Stevens. "I am going to try and get to know the man, observe him, and finally find out enough about him so we can guarantee a conviction."

The men shook hands after Evans gave Stevens his full support and promised to help in any way he could. Both men knew that amidst the carnage of war that Stevens was basically on his own.

When Captain Mark Stevens met Major Roderick Smythe, he took an instant dislike to the man. Smythe was only 5 foot 6 inches in height and had to look up in order to speak to his subordinate. Mark could tell straight away that Smythe objected to him being sent to command a platoon of men where, by rights, it should have been Smythe who appointed the new officer.

"You say you went to the same school as Brigadier Evans?"

"Yes sir," replied Stevens. "I suppose that's why I am lucky to be here." He was being deliberately naive.

"You'll see how lucky you are the first time you have to go over the top and fight for real."

Mark just stood to attention and tried not to show his contempt for a man who, rather than lead his men from the front, always chose to stay behind enemy lines and guide the battle from the safety of H.Q.

It was only he and the four men in London who knew the real reason why he was here to kill this odious man. It had nothing to do with supplying information to the enemy. It had been rumoured that the major, whilst inspecting the new intake of troops almost on a weekly basis, always picked out the youngest lad to be attached to HQ as a runner. The stifled screams coming from the major's quarters of a night suggested that the major had other uses for the young boys. It was also noted that the lads were very quickly sent to the front line with the inevitable results. Mark had to have proof that what had been reported was actually happening, and he aimed to get it from the young lad in his platoon who Mark suspected was the latest in a long line of innocent victims.

Mark looked from his left then to his right to see if his men were ready. The men were quiet apart from the youngest who was quietly sobbing. At 15 years old, and looking younger, Brian Johnston had lied so he could join his brother and his mates on the big adventure to go France, kill a few Germans, and return home heroes. His brother had been killed on the first day by shrapnel from their first shell attack. The burning hot metal completely sheared his right arm off, and he died in his brother's arms with both boys covered in blood from the gushing wound.

Brian hadn't even fired his rifle yet! His blond hair and youthful good looks were obviously the attraction that got him noticed by the major, but now he had served his purpose, and it was his turn to die.

Mark had tried to talk to the lad twice about Major Smythe, but both times the lad had just stood to attention and remained silent. The lad was obviously petrified. Mark knew in his heart that Smythe was guilty, but he had to be sure in his head. He needed evidence from the lad. It was too late now. They were both involved in the assault planned for the day. There was no way out if Mark was to maintain his undercover identity.

****

The First Day of the Battle of Passchendaele

Mark took a strong hold of the shaking young boy. It was imperative that they both survived the day.

"Now listen, son, just stay with me, do whatever I do. We will run for 50 yards, and when the machine gunners get our range, we will take cover. When the guns pass over us, we run another 50 yards and then take cover again. Do you understand?"

The lad looked up at Mark and nodded.

Mark stood tall and blew his whistle as the second hand of his watch reached 6am.

He could hear the sound of similar whistles up and down the line as thousands of men rose to attack the enemy positions.

The platoon's objective was a machine gun nest 400 yards over the swamps and craters of no man's land. The noise of the pre-battle barrage had finished to leave only the sounds of the cracks of rifle fire, the buzz of a million bullets, and the chatter of death from the hundreds of machine guns opening up on the advancing troops. The roars from the throats of the advancing soldiers were created by a mixture of fear and adrenalin and served only to help push them onwards to certain death as the machine guns mowed them down row by row.

Mark dragged the young lad over the top with him and shouted encouragement to the men to his left and to his right. Almost immediately, men started to drop like flies. Some threw their arms up in despair, others stumbled and knelt on their knees before tumbling over. Some were blown into smithereens from the ever-present shells raining down.

Mark and the young lad survived the first 50 yards and took cover in a flooded shell hole. Two bodies from a previous attack lay crumpled, bloodied and broken, and, through unseeing eyes, could only stare at the two new occupants with an air of deathly disbelief.

Mark risked a look above the rim of the shell hole only to be met by a burst of machine gun fire which splattered mud everywhere. Mark turned as a soldier screaming and holding his bullet-ridden stomach, fell into their shell hole. Mark knew he couldn't help the tormented soul as every man was ordered to advance and not to stop for anyone.

With this thought in mind, Mark grabbed the youngster and ran for his life to the next objective 50 yards away.

How they made it, Mark will never know. Through the smoke and the carnage, men constantly screaming for help, thousands of bullets flying through the air sounding like crazy bees, it was complete madness.

They both dived into a shell hole where four men from their own platoon had already decided they had had enough.

"Come on, men. Let's take these bastards out." Mark pointed at the biggest of the four and said, "Right, you come with us two, and we will attack from the left. You three attack from the right. Once we have taken out the machine gunners, we will hold and wait for our relief."

Mark, the young lad, and the soldier ran zig-zagging through the mud. Somehow, the lad had dropped his rifle along the way. Shells exploded all around them and, all of the time, the bullets from the machine gun were seeking them out. The first to get hit was the soldier. A bullet in his throat nearly took his head off, and he fell silently to the ground. Mark pulled the young lad down to see how the other three were doing only to see a single shell explode amongst them. When the smoke cleared, there was nothing but what looked like red rain dropping from the sky.

In desperation, Mark took a couple of Mills bombs from his webbing and ran furiously, ducking and weaving till he was within throwing distance of the machine gun nest. His first throw was short but the smoke from the explosion allowed him to get nearer without being spotted. The second bomb was long and true resulting in a direct hit and the satisfaction of seeing several bodies flying through the air.

Mark dived into the nest swiftly, followed by the young lad. They both surveyed the scene all around them. It was a terrible mess. There was a complete scene of devastation. All around them, there were hundreds of bodies all lying at grotesque angles. Body parts were strewn everywhere with the cries of the wounded rising above the crashing of the shells. Mark was able to stand and call over what was left of his platoon to defend and hold the line that they had so gallantly fought for.

There were several counter-attacks by the Germans that day but, with the help of relief troops, the line was held. When the fighting died down, what was left of Mark's platoon walked back to their own lines for some well needed rest. So many lives lost for 400 yards of mud, blood, and slime.

Mark made a point of feeding the platoon some hot food as soon as was possible. He couldn't get the shocked boy to speak, so he ordered up extra rations of rum for everyone and, between coughs, the lad managed to drink some of the dark sticky liquid and swallow some piping hot soup.

Then, along with the rest of the bedraggled soldiers, the boy somehow managed to fall asleep. Mark stayed awake to keep watch until 2am. He then awoke the platoon sergeant to take over until daybreak. He went over to Brian and gently shook him until he stirred.

"Hey! You did good out there today, son."

"You saved my life. Thank you, sir," replied the boy.

Mark then told the young lad the good news that he would be taking him to England tomorrow, back to his family. The youngster could not believe his ears and asked why he had been lucky enough to be chosen. It was when Mark mentioned the major's name and what had gone on, that the young lad broke down.

"I had to let him do it," cried the lad. "He threatened to have me shot in front of a firing squad because I had lied about my age."

Mark held the lad in his arms till he finally stopped crying and, once again, the boy dropped off to sleep.

14

Passchendaele. October 13th, 1917. 5am.

The sun was just breaking over the horizon when Mark entered the major's dugout and roughly shook him awake. The major's first reaction of anger turned to fear as he realised Mark's pistol was levelled at his testicles.

"We know all about you and your fancy for young lads." Mark was seething with anger. "I am taking you to be court-martialled, and you will be shot for cowardice in the face of the enemy. The truth will be withheld only to protect the reputation of the regiment."

"You have no evidence," stated the major.

"Your latest young lad survived the battle. He will be in the courtroom and, I promise you, will tell everything."

Mark moved closer as he looked the man in both eyes.

"You have two choices to make. I will go outside for a couple of minutes to smoke a cigarette. You can either do the right thing and use your own pistol and blow your brains out, or you can be court-martialled and disgrace your own family. Take your pick."

Mark went outside and smoked his cigarette. He looked at his watch. Five minutes had passed. It was obvious that the cowardly major did not have the guts to do the decent thing. Mark had always known there would be no court-martial.

After waiting another couple of minutes, he took out a Mills bomb, removed the pin, mentally counted to eight, turned, drew back the cover of the dugout, threw the bomb inside, and marched swiftly around the corner to take cover. The muffled explosion told him that the four men in London would be satisfied with the result.

Chapter Two

A Change in Career

June 26th, 2020. Noon.

Jack Stevens was celebrating his 21st birthday in the best way possible. He was flying a Spitz aerobatic aeroplane upside down at 10,000 feet above the English countryside. Two miles below him, 50 guests were helping to celebrate his special day alongside his mother, his sister, Susan, and his girlfriend Louise with a champagne B.B.Q. in the garden of their old rectory on the outskirts of the village of Middleton in Leicestershire. Jack's twin brother, Mark, had already had a family dinner to celebrate his 21st the previous month and was away on duty with the Special Boat Services, so he was unable to attend the B.B.Q. As always, their father was working but had promised he would be along later.

Jack looked at his new watch, an Omega Speedmaster, the birthday present his parents had bought both boys, and waited for the second hand to reach 12 o'clock precisely. When it did so, Jack started the aerobatic routine that he hoped would win him the title at next month's world championship to be held in Las Vegas, Nevada.

Even to the uneducated eye, it was clear to everyone looking skywards that Jack was a superb pilot performing twists and turns, loop de loops, and throwing the small plane around the sky as though it was a rag doll. Jack drew a gasp of horror as everyone in the garden thought he hadn't pulled out of his final dive, only for the Spitz to reappear hedgehopping into the field next to the rectory to make a perfect three-point landing. The birds were able to carry on with their summer chorus when Jack switched off the powerful Prat and Whitney engine, hopped out of the cockpit, and ran to join his guests.

There was laughter when Jack took three attempts to blow out all of his candles on his birthday cake, courtesy of Susan, and after the traditional 'Happy Birthday', thanked his mum, Susan and Louise, for organising the party, and his Aunt Mary for doing the food. He then apologised for his dad's non-appearance due to urgent business. Mark's mum raised a laugh when she said she hoped the 'urgent business' wasn't another woman! As Mark's mum and dad were very happy and had just celebrated their silver wedding anniversary, that was highly unlikely.

Before too long, the sun decided to set behind the tennis court at the back of the garden throwing long shadows over the departing guests. Louise had left early as she had to go back to uni the next day. Jack was alone watching T.V. later on in the evening after his mum and sister had gone to bed when the front doorbell chimed.

Jack made his way to the front of house smiling as he could not remember the last time his dad had forgotten his key.

Jack opened the door. It was not his father standing there. It was two uniformed police officers.

'Excuse me, sir, are you Mr. Jack Stevens?' asked the smaller of the policemen.

"Yes," replied Jack. "How can I help you?"

"It may be better if we came inside, sir."

Jack took the two policemen through to the living room. All three men were still standing.

"I regret to inform you that your father and brother have been in a serious car accident."

The policeman waited for Jack to say something.

"Well, for God's sake man, are they alright?" Jack's heart was racing.

"Your father, Mark Stevens, died of his injuries early this evening, and your brother, Mark Jr., is in intensive care at St. Thomas's Hospital in London."

Jack collapsed onto a chair and buried his face into his hands.

****

The following 10 days were a nightmare for Jack. Although he was the youngest in the family, it was he who had to organise all the necessary details for the funeral. Susan was a complete mess, and his mum hadn't spoken more than two words since she had heard the news. Both women moved into a hotel near Mark's hospital so they could visit him every day, but the lad was in a coma and was on life support, and the doctors were not very hopeful.

Jack spent hours on the phone to Louise, who had to stay at Oxford as she had her finals, but no matter how much he talked, he couldn't get his head round his dad not being there. He had been to visit Mark and sat there for hours holding his hand, talking to him, telling him long forgotten stories of when they were little playing in the woods, anything to try and get a reaction. Nothing!

The twins were so alike when they were small, but when they changed from boy to man, Jack carried on being the funny one, always trying to make people laugh.

Mark turned into a very serious young man. As he was the oldest by ten minutes, he naturally assumed he would go to Sandhurst where his father and his grandfather had gone. A life in the army proved a very successful move for Mark, and of course, he passed his training with flying colours and achieved the rank of captain at the tender young age of 20. Jack went to uni, had a great time, got his degree in media studies, which did nothing for his job prospects, and worked as a milkman to pay for his flying lessons. Although the twins hadn't seen a lot of each other for the past year, they kept in touch on Facebook texting and occasional facetime conversations using the webcams on their computers.

The funeral of Mark Stevens, Sr. had to be delayed as they could not release the body until an autopsy had taken place. The hammer blow of his father's death had completely knocked Jack for six, and it took all of his will just to get through every day. But decisions had to be made about the venue for the funeral, the cars, the catering. Jack completed the necessary tasks with a heavy heart.

When the funeral finally took place at the nearby village church, they had to set up some speakers outside so the service could be relayed to those guests who were unable to get a seat inside. Jack had decided to hold the reception in the garden of the rectory where only weeks before, there had been a celebration. More than 200 people turned up, and once again, Jack thanked his Aunt Mary for doing the catering. There were quite a few of his dad's old army mates at the reception, and one, in particular, asked if he could come and see Jack in the near future. Jack agreed and just assumed it was to do with his dad's army pension.

Once again, the sun chose to set over the far end of the garden, but this time, after all of the guests had gone, it only left Mark and Louise tightly holding onto Mark's mum and his sister who were both sobbing uncontrollably. There was still no change in Jack's brother's condition, and as Jack held the three most precious people in his life, he couldn't believe how his family had been torn apart. One day he had been flying as high as an eagle in a clear blue sky, the next day his whole world had come tumbling down. Jack looked up at the sky and wondered if he would ever fly again.

It was about a week later when the front doorbell chimed once again with Jack alone in the house. He was in the library at his father's desk trying to make head or tail of the computer records. There were dozens of files on his father's laptop, but Jack had no knowledge of any passwords. He could not ask his mum as she was still staying down in London with Susan to be near the hospital. Both women had expressed a desire to be away from the house and all of its memories for a while, and they both still believed that Mark would somehow pull through.

So, Jack had dozens of files on his dad's computer but no access. Even Louise, who was brilliant with computers, could not help as, without the passwords, there was nothing anyone could do.

Jack left his father's office, walked through the long corridor to the front of the house, and opened the front door. He immediately recognised the gentleman who had spoken to him at the funeral.

"Hello again, I'm Commander James, your father's old commanding officer. We spoke at the funeral."

"Yes, I remember speaking to you, sir, please come in."

Both men shook hands, and Mark was immediately impressed with the firm grip and the tall bearing of a man who obviously had spent many years in the military.

22

"How is your brother?"

"Not so good. Still in a deep coma," replied Jack.

Mark took Commander James into the library and asked if he would like a cup of tea.

"Yes, please, black with one. Do you know, Jack, it is years since I have been in your house. I remember Susan had just started school, you were toddling about the floor trying to take your first steps, and Mark, who could already walk, was marching up and down banging on a drum.

"Your twin brother was the fourth Mark Stevens I had met from the same family as I knew your grandfather during the Second World War, and I briefly knew your great grandfather, also called Mark Stevens, who saw action in the First World War."

"Where did you serve with my father?" asked Jack, more out of politeness.

"We were in the Bomb Disposal unit in Iraq and then in Afghanistan."

Jack was puzzled. "I thought my father served his time as a major in the Catering Corps."

"That is why I am here today, Jack, as I am going to tell you a few things about your father's past and your brother's involvement in your father's work, and then I hope you will consider a change in career."

"A change in career? I'm a professional pilot. Why should I think of doing anything else?"

The tall military man sat back in his chair. "I have been authorised by no less than a member of the Royal Family to offer you a new position."

Chapter Three

Revelations

Jack took both empty cups back to the kitchen, rinsed them through, and wondered what the hell the old man was on about.

When he returned to the library, the man was standing.

"I see you have your father's laptop up and running."

"Yes," said Jack. He looked over at the new Apple 3D iPad that he and Susan had bought their dad for Christmas.

"Would it surprise you if I told you I had access to all of the passwords required to open his files?"

"Yes, it would," replied Mark. "I don't even know if my mum knows them."

"I can assure you, Jack, that she does not. You see, your father and I worked for British Intelligence, and, if I was to let you have access to those files, which I am fully prepared to do, you would have to sign the Official Secrets Act before I could do so."

"The Official Secrets Act! What the bloody hell is going on?" Mark was starting to get angry.

The commander then moved to Mark's father's office desk and proceeded to move it sideways to reveal a large metal safe that had been completely hidden from view.

"How the hell did you know about that?" Jack exclaimed.

He was actually quite impressed with the old man's strength as it normally took two of them to move the desk.

"I have always had a set of keys for this."

With that, he took the duplicates from his coat pocket.

"We only ever had one key for the safe. Does that other key open the bottom drawer?" Jack asked. He often had wondered what his father had hidden away in the bottom drawer. He just assumed it was his mum's jewelry or whatever.

"In the old days, our reports and information files were kept under lock and key but now, as you have found out, our latest work is kept on computer."

James bent down to unlock the safe. He took the smaller key and unlocked the bottom drawer. From that he took two large folders.

"Jack, these are you grandfather's and great grandfather's service histories. Their diaries if you like. Because they are over 50 years old, and therefore out of the jurisdiction of the Official Secrets Act, I am going to leave them for you to read. Here is my card, and I am certain you, after reading the folders, will want to know more about the work we do. Feel free to call me anytime."

Jack didn't know what to say as this had all came as quite a shock to him.

Commander James came over to Jack, handed him the two files, and said, "Don't worry, I will see myself out."

When Jack heard the front door close, he sat down in his father's chair and began to read the two volumes of family history he had no idea existed.

Chapter Four

Decisions

Jack decided to start at the beginning and read the oldest file of the two concerning his great grandfather. The first page gave his full name, Mark William Stevens, date of birth, March 1st, 1895, and his rank, squadron leader. This puzzled Jack as he was always led to believe his ancestors were army men, and his father always joked that Jack had broken with tradition when he had insisted that he wanted to learn to fly.

Jack read the first pages, fascinated by the original training methods for teaching men to fly machines that had only been invented less than five years before the start of the First World War. He was impressed to read that the first solo flight was achieved after only five hours and the first patrol after only fifteen. They must have been desperate for pilots to send them to the front line after so little experience.

Jack thought back to the day he passed his flying test when he was only 17.

After his instructor had congratulated him, the man who had sat in the cockpit with him throughout most of his 42 hours, turned to him and said, "Now go out and learn to become an airman."

The First World War pilots did not have the luxury of 42 hours. They had to learn quick as the average life expectancy of a young pilot then could be measured in weeks.

Jack turned to the next chapter in the diary that recorded the thoughts of his great grandfather after he had recorded his first kills.

"I led the dawn patrol at 5am this morning. I took Smith and Brown with me. My squadron had received the new Sopwith Camels only a few days before, and we all needed time in the air to get used to such a beautiful aircraft. Compared to our old Bristol Fighters, the Camel flies like a Rolls Royce, and with twin machine guns firing through the forward propeller, I fully expected the number of kills to increase. Both young men needed the experience. I gave them strict instructions to stay with me at all times. It was our usual job to patrol the lines to make sure the German reconnaissance planes could not photograph the new positions of our troops on the ground.

"Our section of the line was 20 miles either side of our base, so it was a matter of flying up and down keeping a watchful eye for enemy aircraft and always not flying in a straight line to make us a more difficult target for the enemy anti-aircraft fire known as 'Archie'. All of a sudden Smith, flying on my right-hand side and slightly behind me, waggled his wings and pointed furiously downwards. There was a two-seater enemy spotter plane just crossing No Man's Land about 5000 feet below us.

"I turned to point this out to Brown with no intention of immediate action as it was my experience the spotter plane could be a decoy with enemy fighters flying higher than us waiting to strike.

"I was too late as Smith had started to dive towards the target with Brown dipping his right wing to follow him.

"I held back, and sure enough, I spotted a couple of Fokker V5's flying out of the sun following the line of descent to protect their own aircraft. With the advantage of height and superior speed, they would be able to attack within minutes.

"I put my Camel into an impossible dive. At full throttle and at full speed, I had to reach the enemy fighter planes before they attacked and before the wings of my own aircraft were torn off. My near vertical tactic paid off as I was able to get behind the first of the Fokkers and rake his cockpit with a single burst from my Vickers machine gun. The enemy machine immediately went out of control and flames started to lick around the cockpit. All aeroplanes are made of wood, and it didn't take long for them to burn. The pilot had three choices. He could jump to his death, get burnt alive or, if he was carrying a pistol, a single shot to the head would be the quickest way to die with no pain. I hoped the pilot had been killed so he wouldn't be faced with these terrible decisions as, for some strange reason, the powers to be on both sides of the war have decided that only balloon observers could have the safety of wearing a parachute.

30

"I looked around to see what else was happening. Brown was flying low towards our own lines with smoke trailing from his engine. Smith had engaged the second fighter, and they were both circling each other to gain advantage. This was only going to end one way as the enemy plane could turn tighter, so I flew across his line of fire to try and divert him away from the young lad. The enemy plane took the bait and started to try and catch me. I flew lower and lower to try and escape, but the opposing pilot was determined, and I could not shake him off. I heard a burst of machine gun above the noise of my engine and fully expected to feel the thud of the bullets ripping into my aircraft. Instead, I heard a massive explosion, and as I turned round, Smith flew past me with his arm raised in a victory salute. Thank God the lad is a quick learner.

"But there was still the matter of the spotter plane. It had to be stopped at all costs. What was one life compared to the thousands that could be lost if the enemy had advanced photography of our battle plans. I waved Smith to go home as we were miles behind enemy lines and running low on fuel.

"I gave it a few more minutes, and then I spotted it. The enemy aircraft was obviously near home as it was preparing to land, flying slow and level, away from the sun. This gave me all the advantage I needed. I had the height, the speed, the sun behind me, and the element of surprise. The photographer, who sat in the front seat of the two-seater, must have turned round to speak to the pilot and, as doing so, he spotted me. He frantically pointed at me and tried in vain to turn his machine gun around to defend himself and their valuable cargo.

"They had no chance. I had them in my sights and gave them a long burst from both guns straight into the body of the aeroplane. The Fokker was shot to bits and instantly disintegrated. Both men spiralled to their deaths 500 feet below with arms and legs flailing in the wind.

"I immediately increased power and headed back to our own lines. I had a moment of panic as the Camel ran out of petrol on finals to land, but I was able to glide the machine in for a safe landing.

"My emotions were mixed that night as I lay in my bunk with the adrenalin still pumping through me. Brown had managed to get back to the airstrip but had crashed on landing. The explosion, and the resulting fire, was enough to instantly destroy both man and machine. Smith and I had survived to fight another day. I knew now I was a warrior and could kill in the heat of battle. What I couldn't stop thinking about were my feelings when I shot down what was basically an undefended aircraft, killing two men. I knew my actions would save countless lives, but it still kept me awake all night thinking that I was also very good at being a cold-blooded murderer."

****

Jack closed the diary and looked at his watch. It was two o'clock in the morning. He had been re-reading and thinking about the report for hours. Later on, he lay in bed thinking of what his ancestors must have gone through. He couldn't imagine a world where all of the young men were expected to go off to war and die for their country. What was it like to have killed another human being? He finally fell into a fitful sleep.

He dreamt of young boys falling from aeroplanes, screaming, with their clothes on fire.

Chapter Five

Directive

Jack woke early the next morning. It was still dark as he took Lexus, the family dog, for his morning walk. The standard poodle must have wondered what was wrong as his master was quiet in thought, and, before they knew it, they had walked 10 miles instead of the usual five.

Jack showered and dressed and then, once again, sat at his father's desk. First of all, he made a couple of phone calls. He made sure his mum and sister were alright and never mentioned the family diaries to his mum as he had a premonition that she, like him, did not have any knowledge of the family history. The second phone call was to his agent confirming the cancellation of his trip to Las Vegas. His agent stated that he had already issued a press release citing family reasons for his withdrawal from the competition.

He could not get through to Louise's mobile, so he left a short message. It was concerning to Jack that Louise and he might be drifting apart. His father's death had completely changed his outlook on life, and he seemed to have aged overnight. Talking to Louise now was strained, and Jack felt she didn't understand what he was going through. He was going to suggest a holiday in Louise's half term so they could get away and try and get the relationship back on track.

Jack then left the house, walked to the Spitz that was still parked in the adjacent field, and, after spending the normal 20 minutes doing all of the pre-flight checks, fired it up, and flew off to the nearest airport at Sywell, Northamptonshire, to leave the aeroplane there for the time being. Jack just had a feeling that he wouldn't be needing it for the foreseeable future. It was the first time since Jack had started flying that he felt no joy that morning. Getting the aeroplane to its hangar and driving back home was just a task that had to be done so he could get back to reading the rest of the diaries. With a cup of coffee in his hand, Jack once again settled down to read his great grandfather's diaries.

"I have been called to London to receive my medal from His Majesty the King. I am obviously honoured to do this, but I am a little confused as most pilots, when they have reached 10 kills, are presented with their medal in the field of battle. I think I would rather have the ceremony here in France in front of my men than having to go to London. My commanding officer has told me the press will be there, and it will make a good story to boost moral throughout the country. He said I am now known as an 'ace'. This does not mean a thing to me. I suppose it will make a change to read some good news in the daily papers instead of the casualty lists every day. Then again, I cannot wait to see my lovely wife Marie and to feel her tummy to see if our little one is kicking yet. Strangely enough, though, I cannot wait to get back here, to France, as I think my men need me."

Here was another fact that Jack hadn't known about. He didn't know his great grandfather had been decorated during the war. He turned the page to the next diary entry.

"I was invited to dinner after the medal ceremony by the king himself. We ate at the Military Club. I have been there before but never in a private dining room. It was rather strange as there were no staff to wait upon us. It was unusual to see the king of England pour me a glass of wine. There were also two high ranking army officers present and the First Lord of the Admiralty, Winston Churchill. It was Churchill who took the chair.

"'We are here tonight to ask you to join us in setting up a new military intelligence department. A few years ago, before the start of the war, when I was Home Secretary, it was deemed appropriate that Great Britain should concentrate more on the intelligence side of our affairs.

"'I myself, when fighting in the Boer War, used to cycle into Johannesburg heavily disguised to see if I could glean any information from the enemy to help our war effort. There was no doubt in my mind that if I had been discovered, I would have been executed.

"'I have always recognised how valuable information can be in a time of war. The department we set up to deal with enemy agents operating here in our country is known as MI5. We have recruited operatives that are tasked to track down these agents, by any means possible, to stop them collecting information that could help the enemies of our country. The department that deals with sending agents abroad to collect information that could help us in our war effort is known as M.I.6. You must understand that this is highly secretive and a very dangerous line of work.

"'Both departments have been very successful up to now and have the full backing of our government. However, we now feel, and I must stress that no one outside of this room has any knowledge of our proposal, that there is a need for a further department, call it M.I.7 if you will, where we need a man who can deal with situations that are outside of the norm and outside of our usual control situations, for example, where criminals are using the war effort for their own greed. These men are usually highly intelligent, and we are finding it very hard to get enough evidence to bring them to justice. What we want you to do is to investigate these situations, find enough evidence to satisfy the Directive that we have given you, and to sort the matter out.'

"'What do you mean sort the matter out?' I asked, rather naively.

"'We need you to eliminate the problem. If we all agree that these men deserve to die, it will be your job to assassinate them.'

"When I didn't reply due to the fact I was in a slight shock, Mr. Churchill continued, 'We have noticed from your records that amongst your ten kills, you have shot down three reconnaissance planes that were photographing our troop positions. So, it could be said that you were murdering unarmed men. We are asking no more from you than that. There are situations out there that need direct action where possibly a long drawn out court case would be harmful to the morale of the country. If there are men using the war effort for their own ends, and we decide that action is to be taken, it will be your final decision to solve the problem in whatever way you see fit.'

"I replied, 'So I will have the final say.'

"Churchill looked at His Royal Highness who nodded.

"'You will be the judge and the jury.'"

Jack leant back from the desk to ease his back which was starting to ache from staying in one position too long. He could not believe what he had just read. Winston Churchill setting up MI5! He only knew of Churchill because of his "We'll fight on the beaches" speech during the Second World War. He was amazed to read that Sir Winston Churchill, in his younger days, was one of the original secret agents.

Of course, he had heard of MI5, and wasn't James Bond a member of M.I.6.? Mark had never believed in all this 'Licence to Kill' rubbish that they put across in the movies. But he had just read about the formation of the British Intelligence service and a proposal for a top secret organisation to eliminate people who deserved to die but it couldn't be proved in a court of law. Where would you draw the line? Jack had always said that paedophiles should be executed, terrorists should be hung, and child killers and murderers of policemen should be given a lethal injection. With the latest in D.N.A. technology, cases are so much easier to prove nowadays. Could he agree to the killings being carried out today? That was a huge question. He went back to the diary.

Chapter Six

Decision Time

Jack read through several reports of incidents and situations that his great grandfather had reason to deal with on instructions from the Directive. There was a case of a munitions manufacturer made very wealthy by the Great War, who, to make even more money, reduced the quality of the shells he was producing. He would have got away with it if the shells hadn't started to explode whilst still in the guns, killing the English Tommies instead of the intended German targets. Stupidly, the man tried to take a pistol out of his office drawer after he had been exposed. Jack's great grandfather was quicker and shot him in the face. It wasn't always the case that the Directive ended in cold-blooded assassination.

There was a major in the Coldstream Guards who was clearly more loyal to his German ancestors than the country of his birth. Jack's great grandfather unearthed such rock solid evidence, with help from his colleagues from MI5, that the major was tried publicly, found guilty, and hanged for his act of treason in a time of war. I suppose this case was made public to raise morale amongst the population and also send a message out to other would-be spies that their actions would always certainly lead to their own death.

Jack felt slightly sickened when he read the report of the Mills bomb being somewhat casually thrown into a dugout to eliminate an English officer who was using young soldiers for sex. Was it because it was a time of war, of mass destruction, that a man could be so cold-blooded in his actions? How could such operations be sanctioned by the highest authorities in the land? Surely Jack's own father could not be mixed up in all of this?

Jack picked up Commander James's card that he had left on top of the office desk. After his father's old commanding officer had asked Jack to consider a career change, he had handed him his card and let himself out, leaving Jack with his thoughts about recent events. Jack couldn't help feeling his life was about to be turned upside down. He decided that he would read the second file that had been kept in the family safe for all these years before he would call the commander to find out exactly what was going on.

Chapter Seven

The Second Diary

As the next day was a Saturday, Jack decided to get up early and drive the 60 miles to Oxford to surprise Louise. He had finished reading his great grandfather's diaries, and he decided he would make a start on his grandfather's reports on Sunday. He would then phone Commander James for an appointment on Monday.

He took his dad's Lexus sports convertible, and it brought a smile to his face as the in-car D.V.D. belted out old videos of last century's rock groups. His dad's favourites included The Beatles, the Rolling Stones, The Who. Music that Jack had been brought up on and to which he preferred to the current hologram rap culture tribal music that filled the airwaves. His dad's type of music was the reason he had met Louise. It was in an old school retro rock club at uni. Jack was in his final year, and Louise had just started. They got chatting, laughed together about loving such ancient music, and had a great time drinking and dancing the night away.

Jack wasn't impressed when he arrived at Louise's dormitory. She was pleased to see him but was obviously hungover from yet another student Friday night out. Jack made her some breakfast while she had a shower, and they spent the morning at the Ashmolean Museum where Jack learned a little bit about Alexander the Great, the ultimate warrior. After a pub lunch, they went back to Louise's room and made love on her sofa bed. Was it Jack, or was there a lack of enthusiasm about their day together? Louise chatted about her course in politics, disagreed with Jack about the UK's long-term involvement in Afghanistan, and generally talked about her fellow students, most of whom Jack had never met.

On the drive home that evening, Jack's thoughts were confused. Had his father's death changed him that much? He remembered his own uni days with great fondness and obviously the drinking and socialising were a great part of that, but Jack had always concentrated on his flying, convinced that one day he would end up joining the R.A.F. and become a display pilot for the Red Arrows. Flying had always been his first love, but now he wasn't so sure.

When he got home, Jack got changed into his training kit and went for a brisk five-mile run and then spent an hour in the gym. Together, he and his dad had converted one of the outbuildings of the old rectory into a small but effective gymnasium. Jack had to train regularly as he needed to be as fit as possible for his flying. Some of the manoeuvres he needed to practice in his aerobatic routine would be pulling up to 3g on his muscles, so he had to have a good level of strength as well as all round fitness. Jack hadn't trained since his father's death, so it was with an extra edge that he lifted the weights that night.

Jack didn't sleep particularly well and decided to get up early, took the dog for a long walk, and then had a good soak in a really hot bubble bath. As it was Sunday, he made himself a cooked breakfast, had a quick scan through the Sunday morning papers, and then settled himself down at his father's office desk to read the second diary concerning the activities of his grandfather during the Second World War.

September 1942

"My name is Major Mark Stevens. I am 25 years old, and it is September 8th, 1942. I have been asked by my superior officers to keep a diary, in the form of a daily report about my activities when I am working for the Directive. I fully understand that I am now under the laws and regulations of the Official Secrets Act and, as such, these diaries are to be kept under lock and key from everyone including my own family. I am a serving tank commander with the King's Own First Tank Regiment and have recently been recalled to assist with Special Operations."

Mark put his pen down and rubbed his shoulder. His shrapnel wound had fully healed but occasionally it still gave him some gip! How could he put into words an act of cold-blooded murder?

His hand went from his shoulder onto the ribbon that denoted he had won a military medal. His thoughts drifted back to the summer of '42 when he was leading his regiment into battle against a far superior German tank force in northern Africa.

Within minutes, all the regiments carefully-laid plans to attack and hold a strategic bridge for the oncoming infantry literally went up in smoke. Both tanks either side of him in the leading group had been knocked out, and Mark found himself out front with no visual support. He was screaming instructions into his headset to the driver so the tank could be accurately pointed at the advancing enemy. He only had two rounds left, and he aimed to make them count. There was a nearby explosion, and Mark felt a red hot searing burn across his left shoulder. Although wounded, he waited for the smoke to clear and fired on the enemy. The first shot fell short of the leading German Panzer tank, but Mark upped the barrel trajectory a few degrees and successfully blew the enemy tank to bits with his final round.

With only his onboard machine guns firing, Mark still advanced and was amazed when he saw not one, but two, Panzer tanks explode as if one. The answer to the miracle made itself clear when a Spitfire roared overhead, and making a fast tight turn, came back to continue its attack. All of a sudden, the Germans were in retreat, and Mark was able to wait for the rest of the regiment to form up behind him as he drove across the bridge and set up a line of defence the other side to wait for the infantry. Only when he dismounted from the tank and fainted from loss of blood did his crew realise he was wounded. For continuing courage in the heat of battle and his determination to engage the enemy at all costs despite being severely wounded, he was awarded the military medal.

Mark celebrated his 21st birthday the day he got the news about his decoration. He was granted a week's leave, and it was during his time at home that his father asked if he could have a word in private. Mark entered his father's study as though he was going for a job interview and was puzzled by the air of formality. After some small talk, there was a knock at the door and a stranger in the uniform of a Royal Marine entered. Mark's father shook the visitor's hand warmly and extended an invitation to sit next to Mark.

After Mark was introduced to Major James, he turned to his father and asked if there was anything wrong.

"On the contrary," replied his father. "Now that you are 21, we were hoping you might establish a family tradition."

"What family tradition?" asked Mark, still wondering what the hell was going on.

For the next hour, Mark's father explained about the Directive and how it worked only in the time of war. He told his son about the original meeting with Sir Winston Churchill and the work that he had done during the First World War. Now that he was in his sixties, he thought it would be a good idea if Mark would consider carrying on with these special duties.

When his father had finished talking, Mark just sat there taking it all in. It was Major James's turn to speak.

"We have an urgent situation at the moment where we think important information is being passed onto the enemy."

"Why can't my dad handle it?" replied Mark.

"The information is being leaked from a brothel."

"A brothel!" Mark was incredulous.

"We suspect the madam is an enemy agent and as the brothel's usual customer is a teenage squaddie, I do not think your father would blend in."

"If I find out who the culprit is — what then?"

"It will be your job to eliminate the suspect."

"I'll need some time to think." Mark was very pensive about the whole situation.

After Major James left, Mark and his father stayed up until the early hours talking things through, and eventually, they both agreed that his father's actions, notwithstanding the morality of it all, had saved countless lives, and in a time of war, everybody lived by different rules, so there should be different solutions for war-time problems than there would be in peacetime. Mark agreed to start as soon as possible and was soon caught up in the urgency of all the training required. Mark's thoughts then scanned from the time of his 21st, his weeks of special weapons training, learning new skills, basically several ways of killing people without making too much noise, and his lack of sleep about whether he would be up to the job. He had made several visits to the Soho premises which housed the brothel upstairs and a club on the ground floor and was now considered a 'regular'. It was the time in which to make his move.

The normal routine on entering the club was to order a drink from the bar, wait until he was approached by one of the girls, and then, after several rounds of drinks, to go upstairs to one of the bedrooms. On his first couple of visits, Mark complained of a headache to the girls, paid the cash, and left without doing the dirty deed. It was decided that this was no good for his cover and was told in no uncertain terms to 'lie back and think of England.'

Mark already had a steady girlfriend and, thank God, they had decided to wait until the war was over before they got married. Mark would have to feign shyness on his wedding night and withhold all of his newfound skills.

On his next visit, Mark pretended to be drunker than normal and boasted of his preference for older woman and shouted, "Why doesn't the boss ever buy me a drink?"

Martine Escalle was 52 years old, 5 foot 10 inches tall with an incredible figure for a woman of her age. She didn't normally do business with her customers but, on hearing about the young soldier's boast, and seeing he was one of the better looking men in the club, decided to accommodate him. It became a regular thing between them, and it was after the first month, when they were lying in the madam's bed, that she asked innocently where was he based.

Mark had been primed for this moment and told her that he was a tank commander in charge of a brigade of tanks that were training on the Suffolk Downs. He explained that this was why he couldn't get down to London as much as he wanted as he had only a couple of more days before they were all shipped overseas when their training was completed.

The next night, the Luftwaffe extensively bombed the training area of the Suffolk Downs, and it was leaked that there were heavy casualties and a complete brigade of tanks wiped out. The fact that there were no personnel there during the bombing raid and the tanks were all made of wood did not make the headlines.

The next night, he made his usual visit to Martine's. His acting was superb, he made out he was lucky to survive, he had lost his closest friends, and he was being transferred to the King's Own Second Regiment which was based near Cobham in Surrey.

Mark could have killed the agent when he first got into the bedroom but, like his father before him, he wanted to make sure in his head, as well as his heart, that she deserved to die. Mark said his farewells and closed the bedroom door quietly behind him. He waited a few minutes and then re-opened it. In his hand was a small Mauser pistol with a short stubby silencer already screwed to the barrel. There was no sign of Martine. Mark quickly checked the bathroom; it was empty. It was while crossing back over the room that he caught sight of Martine through a louvre door that he thought was a cupboard but was, in fact, a small room. She was huddled over a shortwave radio and was speaking very quietly into a microphone. She was speaking in German. As Mark was fluent in French, Spanish, and German, he had no difficulty in understanding the co-ordinates she was giving over the radio for the enemy bombers. She was totally unaware of Mark's presence as she was wearing headphones and did not hear him approach. Mark looked down at the nape of her neck where minutes before he had been gently kissing a fond farewell. He raised the gun and put a bullet into it.

Jack yawned as he looked at the study clock. Christ! It was 4am. He had been reading his grandfather's diaries for hours. There were still a few answers needed to his many questions. He wanted to read his own father's diaries but without the withheld passwords, he would have to wait. He prayed for a miracle for his brother to recover so that he could shed some light on his involvement in the Directive. He had a feeling that he and his father had been involved in something together. He would call Commander James tomorrow and ask for an appointment to get further details of what he was required to do and maybe, at the same time, get the answers he was seeking.

Chapter Eight

The Job Interview

It was a month after Jack's 21st birthday, and he couldn't believe how his life had changed. He had lost his father, his brother was clinging onto life, his mother barely spoke more than two words, and his sister just couldn't cope with the grief. He didn't really know why he was heading down to London to meet up with Commander James. He had been told to be at the MI5 building by 9am on Monday morning where he would be met. No other details were given. All his enquiries about the cause of his father and brother's accident had been ignored, and Jack got the distinct impression that certain facts were being withheld in the hope that the whole affair was to be swept under the carpet. So, in this frame of mind, Jack was not in the best of moods when the security guard refused him admission into the MI5 building. When Jack got a bit shirty on not being allowed entry, the Guard opened his flak jacket to reveal a light submachine gun.

"Listen, Sonny, why do you think I carry this around with me? Why do you think this building is the only building in London with anti-tank barriers every 10 feet? We are very fussy who comes and goes and, for the moment, you are not going anywhere."

It was then that a small, light-framed, rather attractive blonde girl came out of the building, said to Jack, "Follow me," and opened the rear door of a Mercedes limo and, after settling Jack in, drove off in the direction of the city airport. Jack thought it best to keep quiet and wait until they arrived at their final destination. On arrival at the city airport, the young lady drove Jack direct to the V.I.P. boarding gate where a helicopter was already waiting. Jack was escorted aboard and helped with his seatbelt and was given a set of headphones to wear. These were more for reducing the noise of the engine than communicating with the pilot.

This proved to be the case as the pilot only spoke when he was talking with air traffic control and, when given clearance, the helicopter lifted off into the hover, pointed its nose forward, and accelerated across the airfield. Jack sat back and enjoyed the experience of being flown rather than doing all the work himself. Whilst learning to fly, Jack went on to gain his helicopter licence but only on a small Robinson two seater. This jet powered Gazelle was a different animal, and it only seemed like minutes when they started to descend over the coast and land next to a large detached house overlooking the sea.

Upon landing, Jack was met by a rather effeminate young man about Jack's age, who only nodded and indicated for Jack to follow him up to the house. As they approached a large conservatory attached to the side of the house, Jack could see Commander James sitting at a table drinking tea.

The elder man stood, and pointing at the younger man said, "Ah! Jack, there you are. Come and join me. Let me introduce you to my son, James."

Jack politely shook the other man's hand whilst thinking two things. Who would call their son James when their surname was already James, very strange! Jack also thought that it was the first time he had ever shook hands with a fish! All soft and clammy!

"Hi, pleased to meet you. My friends call me J.J. for short."

J.J. made his way back into the house to leave Jack and the commander to conduct their business in private. Jack sat down at the table, and when asked, said he took two sugars with milk and waited for Commander James to explain just why he was here.

"You must be wondering what the hell is going on."

The old man took a cigarette from a packet on the table, offered one to Jack, which was declined, and inhaled deeply before continuing.

"Can I just say before we start how sorry I am about the death of your father and the grim situation surrounding your brother. I make sure I have a daily update on his condition: no change, I'm afraid."

Jack remained silent.

"Your mother and sister are still staying down in London?"

"Yes sir, for the time being."

"Let me start from the beginning Jack, some of which you will have already gleaned from the diaries you have been reading. During the First World War, your great grandfather was the first officer to be used in the Directive. This, as you know, is sanctioned only at the very highest level in a time of war. When a target is authorised, it is up to the man on the ground to deal with the problem, make sure he is 100% positive about the solution, and carry out the elimination. There have been numerous incidents over the years, some which you have read about, and some that are locked away in your father's computer you are not aware of. The Directive always follows the same pattern. One of the four senior officers will put forward a situation, and it will then be discussed between themselves and then with the agent. Recently, this was your father and your brother."

"My brother! You are telling me that Mark was involved?!" Jack was incredulous.

"It has become a family tradition for the agent to train and prepare his eldest son to take over the special agent's work at the age of 21. Your father started to train Mark earlier this year and, on his 21st birthday, Mark took on a Directive case working alongside your father."

"What Directive case?" asked Jack.

"I am unable to discuss this, or any other details, until I have your commitment to join us and carry on the excellent work that your family, and your ancestors, have performed for their country."

"The excellent work meaning I have to learn how to kill people like my brother and father had to do." Jack was starting to get upset.

"Listen, Jack, take a few days to think about this. It's obviously a lot to take in. Your family has always carried out its duties in a traditional military fashion. I realise the army was never your career choice, but I personally believe it is in your blood, and you can become very successful in helping us find the people responsible for your father and brother's car accident."

"What people?" asked Jack.

"I am only telling you this to give you a little more of the big picture, but your father and brother were assisting MI5 in investigating a foreign drug gang. We are looking for suspects who we can charge with the murder of your father and the attempted murder of your brother!"

Chapter Nine

A Decision is Made

Jack didn't get home until the early hours of the morning after his meeting with Commander James. He was flown back to the city airport where a car took him back to St Pancras, but due to the fact that Jack just sat in a bar most of the evening thinking about his father being murdered and his brother only just clinging onto life because of a bunch of scumbag drug dealers, he missed his train and had to eventually buy another ticket for the midnight milk run. Even when he got home, he didn't go to bed. Commander James had refused to give Jack anymore details about the so-called car accident citing the Official Secrets Act.

If Jack decided to become an agent, all the details would be made available to him. The passwords for his father's computer would be given to him, and Jack would get a clearer picture of what was expected of him.

Jack had thought long and hard about the differences between himself and his identical twin. All through their lives, they had been different. Jack's hair was blonde, and Mark's was dark brown. They never dressed the same. Mark played rugby and squash, and Jack loved his football, tennis, and road cycling. Mark lived his whole life for the army; Jack was never happier than when he was flying in a cloudless blue sky with 100 mile view all around. They even had their birthdays in different months. Mark, because he was the oldest by 15 minutes, always celebrated on May 26th and Jack a month later on the actual birthdate.

To say they were chalk and cheese would be an understatement. They were very close as brothers but didn't go out with the same group of friends, and whereas Jack always had a girlfriend, Mark never bothered, always citing his army career as an excuse. Perhaps he was too busy learning how to kill people. Now his brother was asleep, oblivious to the world in a hospital bed, and Jack had been thrust to the position of head of the family with all sorts of thoughts running around inside his head.

The one major point that was bothering Jack was the subject of personal courage. It took a certain amount of bravery to fly the way he did. Some of the manoeuvres he coaxed out of his small aeroplane would scare most people shitless, but the aerobatics were calculated, he knew he had the God-given talent to execute them, and there was always a huge rush of adrenalin to help.

He could only remember having two fights in his life. They were split up before they got too serious, and both times Jack could remember being scared at the thought of physical violence. He hadn't backed down, and he did not run away, but a schoolyard brawl was a completely different world away from killing another human being even if they were scum. He knew the government would train him to kill, and he knew he would enjoy the physical side of the training as he was supremely fit anyway.

Could he kill someone face to face? Was it in his blood like his ancestors before him? His hatred for his father's killers would help. No need for judge or jury. He would be the one to pull the trigger. Could he do it? It was this thought that kept him awake most of the night. Jack took the dog for a very long walk the following morning; he then spent an hour in the gym shifting weights that he had not attempted before. He used his anger towards his father's killers to spur him on and after his shower and a light breakfast, he telephoned Commander James with his decision

"Good morning, sir," said Jack, when he finally got through. "I have decided to take you up on your job offer. When do I start?"

Chapter Ten

The Training

If anybody had asked Jack Stevens about how fabulous it must be to train as a covert undercover MI5 agent, he would have laughed in their face. For six weeks he had lived off the land all over Europe. He had been in countries whose name he couldn't even spell. One hundred mile forced marches a day were the norm with Iron Man time trials held on a weekly basis to check progress on fitness. Jack's swimming was his weakness, and he was always trailing at the end of the 2.4 event. He would then make up ground during the 112 mile cycle ride and then, finally, always finished in the top three at the end of the 26.22 mile marathon.

If Jack had previously thought he was fit, he was soon aware of how mentally and physically inadequate he was for the task of learning survival skills, combat skills, and how to make the correct decisions in high pressure situations where, most of the time, men's lives were at risk. He could now rock climb up sheer mountain faces in all weather conditions; he also had learnt to shoot to a first-class marksman level with close-up pistols and from up to a mile with sniper rifles. He now knew of several ways to kill using his hands, any type of knife, and far too many acts of poisoning. He really worked hard at his self-defence skills as he fully took on board his advice from his personal trainer that it might be best if he could avoid being killed by any of the above before he learnt how to use them.

For the last week, he had been training with the Special Boat Services concentrating on all kinds of explosives. He now had a knowledge of the three main I.E.D.'s that were used in Iraq. He could recognise the smell of a letter bomb before it was opened, and his training included mortar launching techniques as used in Afghanistan. He was taught how to follow other agents and, of course, how to avoid being followed. He was interrogated by the S.A.S. for two days and was proud to have only given them his name, rank, and number despite being held underwater by two gorillas and screamed at constantly to give information.

One of the other trainees got fed up being shouted at and rather flippantly said to the S.A.S. that, "It was all pretend anyway." The punishment for breaking his allotted cover was a helicopter ride that landed on a playing field behind where the guy's mum and dad lived. Jack was told by the S.A.S. officer in charge that the trainee agent had been taken back to Mummy and Daddy where he belonged as there was no room on the programme for anyone with the wrong attitude. It was the last night before the last day of training. Tomorrow's task would be their final exam.

Jack was huddled in a tent freezing cold with only a t-shirt, joggers, and trainers to try and keep warm. His one man pop up tent was next to useless to keep out the howling wind. Unable to sleep, Jack looked down at the luminous dial of his Omega Speedmaster watch. The time was 4am. All of a sudden, Jack heard the unmistakable far off sound of an approaching Chinook helicopter.

An army boot kicked him in the ribs through the tent, followed by a bellowing scream, "O.K., ladies, rise and shine."

The thud of the twin motors of the Chinook grew louder, and the rotor blades flapped as the chopper prepared to land. Jack and the rest of the trainees mustered outside their campsite. They were surrounded by a platoon of soldiers who hustled them into the landing helicopter.

"You will be briefed upon landing," screamed the sergeant major.

All six of the trainees climbed aboard. There were no seats, so everyone just sat on the floor.

As the chopper took off one of the guys asked, "Does anyone have any idea where we are going?" There was no response.

About an hour into the flight, most of the guys had managed to fall back to sleep. Jack forced himself to keep awake. Although he had no idea where they were going, he knew they were flying due west as the sun had just begun to rise behind them. Through a crack in the door, Jack saw that they had crossed the coast but then the change of pitch in the blades told him they were landing. They approached what Jack had assumed to be the Isle of

Anglesey, and before long, the pilot brought the Chinook to a five foot hover.

The training sergeant, who was sitting in the co-pilot's seat, turned and shouted, "You will be given a pound coin and an envelope containing your orders for today's tasks. Once I have given you these, you will jump from the helicopter and proceed back to London and the main MI5 building entrance by 4pm today. If you arrive late, you will fail. If you have not completed your tasks, you will fail. If you are not successful, do not bother to return as there will not be a future for you in British Intelligence. Do I make myself clear?"

"Yes, Sgt Major!" was the unified response.

One by one, the trainees accepted their two items and jumped from the helicopter. Jack was the last to go, and as he landed, he sussed out where the North Star was, turned, and started jogging east across pitch black terrain. The others just stood and watched, unsure of what to do. Jack was determined to get a head start as, first of all, he would need some sort of streetlight to read what the hell he had to achieve in the hours between now and 4pm that day.

One hour later, with lungs bursting, Jack came across a small road. It made the running a lot easier. It was still heading east, but Jack didn't hold out much chance of hitching a lift as he could see no sign of any distant headlight beam in front or behind him. He had already thought of a good story to help him in his efforts to get a lift. He would tell whoever was kind enough to stop that his mates had left him God knows where after his stag night, and he had to get back to London as he was getting married that very afternoon.

The story worked a treat with an elderly couple who stopped 30 minutes later and squeezed Jack into the back of their Mini. The old dear kept banging on about the youth of today.

Jack smiled when the old man told all and sundry, "It isn't like it was in my day. What the young men need is a stiff 20 mile route march to sort them out."

They both thought it was awful of Jack's mates to leave him so far away from London on the day of his wedding. Jack kept up the pretence by replying that he felt lucky he wasn't naked and tied to a lamp post!

Jack had a real result with this first lift as they were able to take him all the way to the outskirts of Birmingham.

As Jack thanked the couple and waved them goodbye, there was just enough daylight for him to retrieve the piece of paper from the pocket of the jogging bottoms and read the instructions for his tasks that day. Jack couldn't believe what he was reading. There were two tasks to achieve during the day before he got back to the MI5 building at 4 pm. The first one was he had to get a job! Not only that, there was an e-mail address where he had to e-mail the details of his new gainful employment. He had to confirm he had actually achieved the task, and there were also details of a new identity, different background, education, etc. He was even given a different age! Jack knew that the most important part of working undercover was to be able to fit into any given situation, so he had to become a good actor and a brilliant liar to have any hope of achieving any success.

Jack started to run towards the centre of town and, within minutes, came upon a shopping precinct. He stopped at an estate agent after he had spotted a job advert for Leaflet Distributors. On entering the reception, he apologised for his sweaty appearance but explained he was just out jogging and had spotted the advert and as he was a student studying for a chemistry degree, the job would be perfect.

The receptionist explained that the job only paid minimum wage and gave Jack a form to fill in and, as he had already committed his new identity to memory, he handed it back minutes later all filled in. The receptionist then took the form through into a back office and came back to ask Jack if he could start that week. Jack nodded. The receptionist disappeared for a further couple of minutes and came back to inform Jack to report for work the next day at 8am. Jack smiled and confirmed that would be great but could the young lady do him a favour and e-mail acceptance of the job to the e-mail address he had filled in on the form as his point of contact?

He went on to explain that the university would need to know as Jack didn't want his grant affected if they thought he wasn't declaring his proper earnings. The young girl responded to Jack's honesty and said she would do it straight away. Jack shook her hand and pleasantly said how much he was looking forward to working with her. Jack smiled and left the office only to pause to tie up a shoelace as he glanced through the estate agent's window to watch, and make sure, the girl had e-mailed the form as requested.

Jack had quite enjoyed the game of pretence and was pleased he had achieved the first task. He only hoped that a part-time leaflet distribution agent qualified as a proper job.

He looked up at the estate agent's sign to remember the number so he could ring tomorrow to give his apologies for his non-appearance. He didn't want anyone to investigate too deeply into his new, although temporary, identity. The next task was going to test his acting and lying talents to the limit. His second task was the biggie! It required him to arrive at London with a reefer of marijuana in his possession!

Chapter Eleven

The Second Task

Jack felt the pound coin in his pocket. Where was he going to buy drugs in Birmingham in broad daylight with only a quid to his name?! By this time, Jack was really hungry, so he stopped at a fruit stall and bought a couple of bananas. He pocketed his forty seven pence change and, after asking directions to the nearest pub or club, walked further into the city centre to see if he could find one which might be open early. Jack was in luck. As he walked past the Blue Angel nightclub, one of the fire exit doors opened to reveal an elderly man carrying rubbish bags.

"Excuse me, mate! You haven't got a toilet I could use? I'm dying for a pee!"

Jack's best smile worked as the old boy said, "Hang on a minute. I'll just get rid of this, and I'll show you where they are."

A couple of minutes later, after climbing a couple of flights of stairs, the old boy led Jack across a litter-strewn empty dance floor and pointed to the gents.

"Cheers, mate!" Jack responded cheerfully.

He couldn't believe the smell of the place and, as he walked towards the toilets, he thought his trainers were going to stick to the carpets! It was enough to put him off beer for life! Whilst he was in the toilet, he took the opportunity to have an all over wash and a long drink from the cold tap of the sink. He looked at his watch. Ten o'clock! He better get a move on if he had any chance of getting back to London before 4pm.

He spotted the cleaner and shouted over, "Thanks!"

When the cleaner looked over, Jack suddenly had an idea and asked the old man where the manager's office was. The cleaner nodded towards a door to the right of the main bar. Jack approached it and respectfully knocked.

"Come in!"

Jack entered into a very small room containing a small desk and an even smaller man sat behind it. He stood up to shake Jack's hand and asked him to sit on the only other chair in the small room.

"Hi, I'm Big Jake, what can I do for you?"

Jack suppressed his sudden desire to burst out laughing and blurted out, "Hello, my name's Jack. I was just wondering if you had any student discount tickets for the club. I'm the social secretary at my uni this year, and I am sure I could fill your club on a mid-week night if I got the right deal. What do you think?"

"Sounds good," replied Jake. "Any ideas on what you would call your night?"

Jack had to really think on his feet. He was not really a nightclub kind of guy and, to be honest, couldn't really tell you the difference between house and hip-hop.

"It would be an old school retro rock night featuring all the stadium bands of the last century: The Stones, The Who, all that sort of music."

Jake looked surprised. "Do you think that would work?"

Jack replied, "Oh! Yeah! Everyone in our first year at uni is mad for it. They're fed up with all the modern rubbish. It will be packed, trust me!"

Jack went on to talk about how he could get the media department at uni to design the flyers and posters for the Retro Rock Night at no cost to the club, and after agreeing to split the ticket money on the night 50-50, Jack stood up, shook the small man's hand and said he would be in touch.

Jack paused as he left the room and turned rather sheepishly before saying, "This is quite embarrassing! A lot of my friends were asking if I could locate anyone who could provide some drugs." Jack held his hands up and continued, "Nothing heavy, just some marijuana for personal use, that sort of thing."

"No problem," said Jake, "our head doorman Chris can help you there."

Jake proceeded to find a piece of scrap paper and wrote a mobile number down on it. As he handed Jack the information, Jack managed to give his most embarrassed look and asked if he could possibly use the club phone as he had come out without his wallet and mobile. Minutes later, after a brief, rather terse, conversation, Jack had agreed to meet Chris at the nearby Weatherspoon's Pub at midday.

"Thanks a lot, Jake, I'll be in touch with the flyers and the posters. I'll ring you, OK?"

"Cheers!" said Jake. Minutes later, Jack had left the Blue Angel nightclub and was sitting in the Weatherspoon's Pub waiting for a noon appointment with a drug dealer!

Jack spent 40p of his money on a pint of tap water with lime and was nursing it when a guy walked over to him and said, "Are you Jack?"

Chris the doorman stood over Jack, obviously trying to intimidate him.

Jack stood up, put out his hand and said, "Hi, you must be Chris. We'll be working together soon."

Jack then went into a load of spiel about he was to be the new promotions manager at the Blue Angel and his first event, The Retro Rock night, would be starting soon every Wednesday night, and Jack was convinced it was going to be really busy and how many doormen did Chris think they would need. This took the wind out of Chris's sails as he supplied the doormen to most of the city centre venues in Birmingham, and he was always looking for more work.

"I thought you were looking to do a bit of business." Jack looked innocently at Chris as they both sat down.

"Oh yeah! That as well. All the students that are into that will be looking to me to provide their needs, if you get my drift. Are you able to supply?" Jack lowered his voice as he took another sip from his drink.

"I can get you anything you need, but how are you going to pay?" Chris was still very sceptical about Jack.

"Well, I thought we could go into partnership. I'll split everything down the middle 50-50, and I would cover Jake's end of it as well. If you could just cover the start-up costs of buying the initial supply, I can pay you back on the first night at the club."

"You mean you want me to raise all the money, and you get half of the profits."

"Yeah! But I will be doing all the selling, I will cover all the promotion costs on all the events at the club, and I will be dealing with all the customers. You don't have to do anything."

Chris was obviously not the sharpest tool in the box and took a couple of minutes to think about what Jack had offered.

"OK," said Chris, "we've got a deal." Both men shook hands and Chris got up to leave.

"Chris?" The doorman turned and sat back down.

"You haven't by any chance got a sample on you, have you?"

"What do you want that for?" asked Chris.

"Well, I've got to go back to uni now and start promoting my new night at the club, and as far as the other business goes, I thought they could try before they buy as an act of good faith."

"How much do you need?" asked Chris.

Jack was stumped. He had no idea what size a pack of marijuana came in. He then had a brain wave.

"Just enough to be going on with, and if I get pulled by the Old Bill, I can say it's only for personal use."

"Sounds reasonable," said Chris, "Don't forget you owe me, and I never let anybody off with a debt, understand?"

With that, Chris passed a small package to Jack, stood up, and left the pub.

Jack couldn't believe it. He was in possession of drugs in the centre of Birmingham at half past 12 in the afternoon, and he had to be in London by 4 o'clock. He finished his drink, left the pub, and headed for New Street Railway station to see if he could blag his way onto a train into Euston.

Getting on the train was surprisingly easy. There were no barriers, and Jack was able to get a seat in one of the quiet coaches. His plan was to immediately appear to fall asleep, so when the conductor came around to check the tickets, Jack, hopefully, wouldn't be disturbed. The real problem would arise when the train finally arrived in London where there were barriers where Jack would need a ticket to get through. Jack would just have to deal with that problem when he got there. Jack knew he was screwed when the ticket collector, a young black girl, woke a guy up two rows in front of him and asked to see his ticket. When the young girl asked Jack, she was a bit confused when Jack asked her to sit down for a minute as he would like to explain why he didn't actually have a ticket.

Jack used all of his charm to describe the fictitious stag night, waking up somewhere in Wales all alone, and his determination to get back for his wedding despite having no money and no mobile phone. Jack went on to explain about the kindness of the people he had met, the old couple who had gave him a lift to Birmingham and, if it wasn't for the 4pm deadline, he would have hitchhiked all the way home. He needed to use the train to have any hope of being on time.

Jack was in luck as half-way through his totally unbelievable story, the young girl started to laugh exclaiming she had "heard it all now."

"When you get off the train, wait for me at the barrier, and I will escort you through the staff exit."

Jack grabbed her hand and kissed it in gratitude. Jack sat back and relaxed. He would be in London with an hour to get to Millbank. He didn't know how far the MI5 building was from Euston, but he was confident he could jog there and still be on time. Jack had actually enjoyed the day.

Thinking and to being able to lie impulsively seemed to come natural to him. What amazed him was how real it all seemed. Half of him was expecting to start work tomorrow as a leaflet distributor for an estate agent, and the other half was looking forward to running a really busy Rock Night at the Blue Angel nightclub in Birmingham. He knew he had come across as totally convincing to everyone he had lied his head off to. Even the young ticket collector was drawn into the fiasco.

Jack had done all the physical training to become an agent. He was as fit as he had ever been, and he felt mentally sharp. He was confident of his self-defence skills if he became involved in a violent situation, but it had become apparent to him today that it was to be his newfound acting and bullshitting abilities that were to be his biggest strength in an undercover situation. He had become totally immersed in his role today and, to be honest, he had got a real buzz from it all.

But always, at the back of his mind, he was worried about that final worst case scenario that his ancestors had faced. Could he kill a man, if directed to, by the powers to be? Today had been nothing in terms of danger. He hadn't even been that bothered when Chris, the doorman, had tried to be the hard man. Jack had just pattered his way out of it. But there would be a time when his new fly by the seat of the pants strategy would not be enough to get him out of a difficult situation.

After Jack had been escorted through the ticket barrier at Euston station, Jack thanked the young girl, headed off to the nearest toilet to grab a drink of water, and started jogging in the general direction of the River Thames. Jack made good time and arrived 15 minutes early to be met at the main gate of the security building by the same armed guard who had been a bit shirty with Jack on his first visit.

"Congratulations, sir! You are the first one to arrive. The commander is waiting to debrief you at reception."

The guard held the door open, and Jack climbed up the small set of stairs where he was met by Commander James.

"Well done, Jack. We received the e-mail confirming your offer of employment and, assuming you have the other item, I will take you through to the debriefing room where you can write out your report of your day's activities."

Jack had arrived back with seven pence left from his original pound coin, he had proof of a job offer, a small amount of marijuana, and the mobile phone number of one of the main drug dealers in Birmingham. Not bad for a day's work. When Jack finally arrived back at Middleton in the early hours of the next day, he was totally shattered. He made a mental note to call Louise in the morning and also to make sure his mother and sister were still bearing up.

He said a silent prayer for his twin brother, Mark, in the hope that a miracle would happen: Mark would wake up, fully recover, and help Jack avenge their father's murder. Jack sat drinking some hot chocolate before he went to bed thinking about the legacy his father had left him, and, uppermost in his mind, now he was a fully qualified undercover agent, what secrets were locked away in his father's computer that might help Jack discover what lay behind his father's death and, ultimately, how Jack could find the culprits and eliminate them.

Chapter Twelve

The Drug Dealer

Scott Parker was celebrating his 40th birthday party. His wife, Harriet, had decked out The Roof Garden nightclub in North London and had invited 200 guests, and Scott didn't even have an inkling it was going to happen.

He thought they were just going out for a meal, and when Harriet said she just had to pop into the office to pick her laptop up, he thought nothing of it. The Roof Garden was special to Scott as it was the first of his four nightclubs that he had bought about 10 years previously. He and Harriet still had their main head office here. He had managed it himself in the early years. He employed the staff, booked the live bands, and he even hosted the karaoke quiz nights. He loved it and, in the early days, often dreamed of owning a chain of clubs up and down the U.K.

Here he was now celebrating his birthday years later, and he had achieved his ambition. He had clubs in Manchester, Birmingham, and Glasgow, and every one of them made good money. The reason was that very early on in his business career he had discovered that selling beer, although quite profitable, wasn't going to be the answer to his dream. The only way to make great money in the nightclub industry was to sell beer alongside a very lucrative side-line, and that was to deal in drugs.

Not only did he supply his own outlets, but through his national security company which supplied doormen to pubs and clubs, security stewards to Premiership football games, and admission security to most of the music festivals, he was able to build up a chain of supply and was able to feed the illegal cash profits through a number of legitimate offshore companies. Scott had a strict rule. He only dealt with what he saw as leisure drugs. Ecstasy tablets and marijuana came in from Amsterdam, and his cocaine came in from South East Asia. He never dealt in heroin or any other hard drugs.

His main success was that he had distanced himself and his family from the ground floor activities, and it only necessitated a bi-annual visit to his holiday villa in Phuket, Thailand, to keep his core suppliers sweet. His regular supply from Amsterdam was dealt with by a standing order, would you believe!

Scott looked around at all the guests at his party as they all sang 'Happy Birthday' after his unsuccessful attempt to blow out 40 candles in one go.

There were two members of Parliament, with their wives and friends, and a well-known presenter of the latest 'Get me Out of Here' celebrity show. Harriet had invited a sprinkle of top class models to satisfy the paparazzi that waited outside the entrance to the nightclub, and there were official photo-journalists from OK magazine on hand and who would be picking up the tab for the champagne that evening.

Scott turned as his son John called for everyone's attention through the club's P.A.

"And now, ladies and gentlemen, the moment you have all been waiting for, live on stage, the one and only Holly Anne Parker!"

A massive round of applause greeted the tall, beautiful, blonde daughter of Scott Parker as she took to the stage, sat behind the grand piano, and began to play Chopin's fifth concerto. You could hear a pin drop. The girl was world class and soon became as one with talent and her instrument. When she finished, the crowd went daft. She was quickly joined onstage by a double bass player and percussionist, and soon proved herself to be a fabulous vocalist and, half-way through a Michael Buble medley of hits, she invited everybody onto the dance floor.

As Scott and Harriet swayed to the smooth rhythms of the band, Scott could not have been prouder. His son John was in his final year to become a doctor, and his daughter had a gig coming up at the Albert Hall with the Royal Philharmonic Orchestra. He had a beautiful wife, a fabulous family, and his business was going well. He was accepted into the upper echelons of London society, and it was rumoured that he would soon be honoured for his charity work abroad which had all started when he had witnessed the horrors of the tsunami in Thailand and had queued the day after, amongst thousands of bloated bodies, to give blood at the local hospital. Who was to know he was in Thailand that Christmas to secure another major drugs supply deal? It was true he had set up the charity to help rebuild the lost homes and businesses of the Thai people, but Scott was very careful not to let anybody have a hint of where his money originated from.

As Scott danced the night away, he nodded over to one of his son's friends, J.J. had been at Eton with his son John and they had maintained their friendship to the extent that, unknown to his father, Commander James, J.J. now worked for Scott.

It had to be said J.J. was a beautiful man. The other men in J.J.'s life had to admit that even most good looking women had nothing compared to the stunning good looks of the young 22-year-old. His long blond hair, piercing green eyes, and an incredibly fit body, honed by hours in the gym, put him streets ahead of the other guys.

Unfortunately, J.J.'s weakness was also his secret. He was addicted to cocaine. The white powder ruled his life. First thing in the morning he needed to cure the blinding headaches that only a couple of hours of fitful sleep would achieve. He had no appetite at the best of times, so a coffee and a croissant, his usual early morning line, and he was ready to go.

J.J. found that a couple of hours in the gym of a morning helped with the headaches and certainly improved his mood. He needed to be in a fit state of mind in case he met up with his father. J.J. despised him. After his mother died of cancer, things got worse between them and, even though they still lived together in the beautiful house overlooking the English Channel, there were enough rooms for them both to avoid each other. The only time they had dinner together was when his father had important guests, and it was deemed that a show of family unity was imperative to his father's image. J.J. was aware of his father's involvement in British Intelligence and would sometimes help with the meet and greet when a new agent would come to the house for meetings with his father.

It was at a recent meeting that J.J. first noticed Jack Stevens. Jack didn't come across the same as the other men that normally came to the house. There didn't seem to be a hardness about him. Perhaps a certain degree of innocence? J.J. was tempted to invite Jack out for a night out with him at a party he had been invited to that weekend. It was rumoured that Holly Anne Parker, the young lady who had invited J.J.'s crowd, was indeed connected to drugs. J.J. was always prepared to deny these rumours, as he worked for Scott Parker collecting the money from his drug sales. It wasn't a good idea to 'bite the hand that fed him'.

Ten hours of solid partying with booze, Ecstasy, and some fabulous looking young ladies would soon sort him out. Maybe some nice looking young men might be his taste? The party that weekend proved to be a washout. J.J. politely stayed for a couple of hours and listened to Holly Anne's gig. He was extremely pissed off after going to the gents toilet wanting to snort a much needed line of cocaine, only to find the security guys at the party had sprayed the cisterns with W.D.40 making it impossible to spread out the cocaine in order, using his credit card, to chop it into lines. J.J. had to agree it was a smart move and helped dispel the rumours of Scott Parker's involvement in drug trafficking, but it didn't do his current needs any good.

So there he was, at midnight on a Friday night, completely sober and bored out of his brain. He made his excuses to Holly Anne, texted a few of his cronies to see where the action was, and left.

Chapter Thirteen

The Final Diaries

Jack's first official day at work as a member of MI5 was actually spent at home. Part of his employment contract meant he had to sign the Official Secrets Act and, as such, Commander Jones gave Jack a set of passwords that would finally unlock his father's diaries. Jack was expected to come up to speed and assist in the tracking down of his father's killers and, he assumed, help stem the all too obvious supply of drugs coming into the U.K.

It was with a strong sense of pre-perdition that Jack switched on the iAir Apple Mac computers in his father's office. It took Jack a while to suss out which password fitted which file but finally one opened up in front of him to reveal the title 'Afghanistan'.

Jack settled down to read about the activities of someone who was not a dimly remembered ancestor but a human being who, only up to a couple of months ago, was a loved and respected father, not a person who had been a secret agent murdered by drug dealers. The diary read as follows:

'To whom it may concern'
"My father, Mark Stevens Senior, had served honourably in the Second World War and had been

decorated twice. I decided to follow in his footsteps and, after leaving university, I trained to become a Royal Marine and was finally accepted into the Special Boat Services. Imagine, to my surprise, on my 21st birthday, I was given my grandfather's and father's diaries to read, and along with these, the option to carry on the family tradition of carrying out certain Directives in time of war to maintain the success of our national security.

I had seen action in Basra during the Iraq campaign and had served two terms of duty there. I was offered my new position by Commander James who, amongst other duties inside British Intelligence, was also an aide to the Royal Family.

I was asked to go undercover in Afghanistan to try and find a way to stop the lucrative drug trade that was largely responsible for financing the Taliban war effort. A top Pakistani politician was rumoured to be involved and, if this was true, it would create a very sensitive political situation. I immediately recognised the man's photograph: he used to be a well-known sportsman, and it was also confirmed to me that the man was indeed engaged to one of the U.K.'s top super models.

After long discussions with members of the Directive, it was agreed the best way to infiltrate was to join a band of British mercenaries who were illegally training young Taliban soldiers in northern Pakistan.

The authorities allowed this to continue as they had a young sergeant working undercover who was already providing valuable information on the movements of the Taliban forces.

It would be hard to describe to the people from England the conditions that these people had to live in. The mountainous terrain meant travel was very difficult, even driving 4x4's, and it took me several days before I reached the camp. The leader of the Taliban, who answered to the name Tabak, was very suspicious, but the young sergeant had already explained I had valuable skills in mortar bombs and other explosives which I could pass on to the young men.

I had to wait several days before Tabak told me there would be a special visitor who was to assess the progress of the new recruits, and I was to be responsible for organising a demonstration of the newly acquired mortar bomb skills.

The assessor arrived at dawn with his driver in an open top Jeep and had an early breakfast with the Taliban chief in Tabak's Bedouin type tent.

I had selected one of the more intelligent recruits to demonstrate his mortar bombing skills, and when asked, the young lad was given a chosen target of an abandoned truck about a mile from the camp.

To everyone's pleasure, the lad blew the truck up with his third shell.

The assessor then shook everyone's hand. He even shook mine and congratulated me on my good work to help get rid of the Western oppressors that were trying to take over their country.

It was ironic that these same Western oppressors gave the man a fantastic lifestyle.

I had persuaded Tabak that it would be a good idea if I escorted the assessor away from the camp the next morning as I and the young sergeant had supplies to fetch for the next bunch of recruits that were due that day for training.

Unbeknown to anyone, on my second night of training, I had got up at four o'clock in the morning, walked a mile down the approach road and had, quite ironically, placed one of the camp's own roadside explosive devices.

The day the assessor left, I made sure I followed his Jeep at a respectable distance. When the vehicle approached the marker I had placed at the side of the road, I dialled the pre-programmed code into my mobile phone and pressed 'Send'.

The explosion was immediate and deadly. Both bodies were blown in separate directions, and the young sergeant confirmed on his side the dead mutilated body of the assessor, and from my side of our Jeep, I could see quite clearly that the driver was beyond help. The fact that she was female and had beautiful long black hair did not bother me. Many a female British soldier would die before this conflict could be resolved.

I took the Jeep to its maximum speed as I knew the explosion would bring an armed response from the camp. I was worried that the pre-arranged helicopter rescue would not get to us in time. The young sergeant was the first to spot, in the blackness of the night, the distant outline of the twin engine Chinook, flying low, scanning the road for our signal. Radio silence was imperative, so I flashed the headlights twice and pulled over. It was only when we were safely aboard that I allowed myself the luxury of looking back to see the enemy's headlights in the distance on their futile chase to catch us."

Jack finished reading the report in two minds. One mind was impressed by the bravery and coolness of the undercover soldiers who did their work under immense pressure.

The other mind could not stop thinking of the detached view his own father had taken coldly killing a young woman. Jack knew he was in for another sleepless night.

Chapter Fourteen

The Mistress

Scott Parker had been sitting in his Bentley G.T. Continental Convertible for over an hour. He had sent his driver home because when Scott went to visit his mistress, it made sense to keep it as discreet as possible. Scott had listened to the message on his smart phone 20 times. After each listen, his heart had grown colder.

Krystal, who was 15 years younger than Scott and was considerably better in bed than his wife Harriet, had had enough. Fed up with playing second fiddle to everything else in Scott's life, Krystal had left a message saying she was seeing someone else and for Scott not to call her again.

There were three phones in the car. One was fixed into the console and handled all of Scott's legitimate business calls. Number two was the personal iPhone inside his jacket pocket that was for only friends and family. The last phone was the latest hi-tech satellite phone hidden inside the armrest that Scott used for all of his illegal activities. This was the number he used to keep in contact with his mistress.

Krystal lived in an apartment in Kensington, costing Scott £2K a month, she drove a B.M.W., worked part-time as a lingerie model, and was to be always available whenever Scott rang to arrange a meet. This arrangement had worked really well for a couple of years, and Scott thought Krystal knew the score. Scott would never leave his wife and family, and in exchange, Krystal had a fantastic lifestyle.

The message on the phone that night had changed everything. Krystal had obviously met someone who could give her more than Scott was prepared to give. She knew Scott would never leave his family, and she had decided to move on.

Scott was cold with fury. He had his life exactly how he wanted it. He had absolute power over his business, his family, and his sex life. No one, but no one, was going to tell him what to do.

Every time Scott listened to the message, he would call a different friend of Krystal's, or work colleague, to find out what the hell was going on. Krystal's phone constantly went to answer phone, and Scott's heart was growing colder by the minute. At last, one of the girls Krystal worked with gave Scott the information he needed. Apparently, she had agreed to go out to dinner that evening with a well-known show biz reporter whom she had only recently met at a photo shoot.

Scott then did two things. He started the car and, at the same time, released the lock on another concealed compartment. He put his hand inside and felt the cold steel of the small Beretta pistol. He checked to see if it was loaded, with the safety catch on, and put it into the inside pocket of his jacket. Scott wanted to find out if the show biz reporter would still be keen to see Krystal if he had a barrel of a gun shoved down his throat.

Finding Krystal wouldn't be too difficult. She had expensive tastes. She was always banging on about why Scott wouldn't take her to The Ivy restaurant. Obviously being one of London's top venue's, it was far too public to display your mistress, and Scott only went there with his family which always really upset Krystal.

It took Scott about 30 minutes to reach the restaurant. Michael, the maître d' always parked his car for him.

"Good evening, Mr Parker, just a table for one tonight?"

"I won't be staying, Michael, I just need a quick word with a couple of friends."

Scott surveyed the room. Krystal was nowhere to be seen. If she was there, she would be upstairs in one of the private dining rooms. Scott grabbed an opened bottle of champagne from a startled waiter and quickly climbed the stairs.

He knew it. They were in the first room. Holding hands, looking into each other's eyes, they didn't notice the 'waiter' approach them. It was only when Scott started to top up their glasses that Crystal looked up with a look of horror, and her new partner looked up with a puzzled expression on his face.

"What's going on?" he asked.

"I'll tell you what's going on, bud. I'm here to help drink to your continued good health and happiness." With that, Scott pulled up a chair.

"I won't be staying long." He turned to face Krystal. "Just long enough for you to give me my keys for the car and my apartment."

"You can't do that." This was the worst thing the young man could have said.

"Listen, Fuckface, I do anything I want, whenever I want to do it. You have a simple choice. You can sit there like a good boy whilst Krystal finds the keys or, instead of dessert, you can eat this fucker!"

Scott shoved the Beretta into the left cheek of the horrified reporter and cocked the trigger. It was obvious the young man had never been threatened by a gun before as, apart from Krystal rummaging in her bag desperately for the keys, the only sound that could be heard was the stream of urine running down the reporter's leg onto the highly polished wooden floor.

Krystal finally handed the keys over.

"Have a good life bitch and think yourself very, very lucky that I don't give a shit for you, and never have done, or you would be sitting there with a hole in your head.

"As for you, 'Clarke Kent', don't ever breathe a word of this to anyone or think about printing anything about me or my family in your shite newspaper. Understand bud?!"

91

The young man nodded and started to sob quietly.

Scott spent the rest of the night in Peter Stringfellow's nightclub. He needed a new mistress sooner rather than later.

Chapter Fifteen

The Drugs Run

J.J. was careful his father never met any of his circle of friends. They certainly wouldn't have met with his approval. The one J.J. trusted the most was Boz, his driver and minder. Anything J.J. needed doing, Boz would organise it.

Most times when J.J. would say, "Right, we've got this to do today," Boz would come right back at him, "That's sorted already, boss."

Boz was originally from Croatia. He had lost both parents during the horrific war with Serbia, so he had made his way to the U.K. to stay at his father's sister's house. At the age of 15, he never bothered going back to school. He was already fully grown at six foot two inches. He scraped a living doing bits and bobs, mostly labouring on building sites. This built his muscles up to the point he was spotted in a local nightclub where the manager asked him if he would like to join the team of doormen he employed to keep the trouble out of his club.

Boz took to this like a duck to water. He only had one rule with the troublemakers. He would ask them once, and only once, if they would kindly leave the nightclub in peace. If they weren't to do that, he would bar them for life. This threat worked with most punters. The guys, and sometimes girls, who ignored his advice were lifted off their feet, carried to the entrance of the nightclub, and physically thrown out onto the street. Growing up in this environment, he soon learned to take care of himself although he had a few scars caused by knife wounds. He actually took a gun off a punter once before throwing him out. When he took the firearm to the police station, he was informed it was only a starter pistol. Boz informed the police that his arse didn't know that at the time.

When he met J.J., he was the ideal man for the activities J.J. was involved in. J.J. was responsible for collecting the drug money off the feeder pubs to Scott Parker's nightclubs. J.J. had a man at each feeder pub door, and J.J., with Boz as his minder, would trawl the pubs different nights of the week to pick the money up and see that the dealers had enough stock. It was only lately that J.J. had been given the opportunity to move into the big league dealing in heroin. He had been contacted on his mobile phone by a man who was obviously using some form of electronic device to mask his real voice. He lay awake all that night wondering who the man was, how did he get the number of his personal mobile phone, how did he know what he did for a living?

He was given instructions which were followed the next day with a jiffy bag envelope with £5K stuffed into it in used notes. For five grand, J.J. soon stopped wondering who he worked for. That was serious money. All he had to do was to take the drug money to the drop off point and pick up the goods. The money was delivered to J.J.'s house that evening. A million pounds all wrapped up in a cardboard box.

Perhaps it was best if he didn't know who was his new boss. He now knew that his new job had nothing to do with small time nightclubs. He was going to be dealing with the big boys. This new line of business meant he was going overseas so, what was needed was a mode of transport that would be very difficult to trace. A helicopter, of course.

J.J. was a lover of fast exotic cars and very expensive flying machines. So, it was quite a come down for him to ride a B.M.W. motorcycle. He kept it next to his father's Mercedes in the family garage that used to be the stabling block for the horses that were needed before the invention of the motor car. His father never asked J.J. about his mode of transport; in fact, he never asked his son about anything, as they very rarely spoke. Commander James knew when J.J. was going 'into town' as he was always picked up by his driver, some chap called Boz driving a Jaguar. The only thing that bothered Commander James about his wealthy wife dying of pancreatic cancer was the bitch had left all of her money to J.J. Why J.J. still lived in the old house was never discussed.

No one was to know that the B.M.W. helped J.J. travel where he wanted to without being recognised. That night, he had travelled the 22 miles by the fourth route to ensure he was never followed.

With Boz as his pillion passenger, both men wore all black motorcycle outfits, black boots, and black crash helmets. The black visors completed the disguise. They had five different routes to take until they came to three acres of old allotments that J.J. had bought a few years back with one thing in mind. To hide his quarter of a million pound Augusta 109E helicopter. There was no road, or even a track, to the old disused farm building two miles away that, from the outside, looked as though it was about to collapse any minute. Both guys walked through the long grass in the dead of night, approached the building, and J.J. clicked a remote which silently opened a small hatchway to the rear of the building. Once inside, he clicked the remote to close the door and, when he heard the satisfactory click, he turned on the light switch to flood the inside of the barn with a multiple of floodlight L.E.D.'s.

There stood in all its magnificence the Augusta 109E helicopter. It was painted in black, leather seats and interior in black, even the rotor blades and engine were painted black so the aircraft would be impossible to spot.

Before they got into the machine, both men removed their Waltham PK 25 pistols from their holsters. They swapped guns and both men checked each other's armament. Satisfied they were locked and loaded, they swapped back. J.J. didn't believe in leaving anything to chance. If the delivery went pear-shaped, he needed to know they could shoot their way out of trouble.

The barn doors remained shut as J.J. did all the necessary inside and outside checks. He fired up the two C120 cyclonic jet engines and, aided by the neon blue of his instrument panel, he waited for the engines to reach their required temperatures and the rotor blades to reach their operating speed.

He checked Boz had his headset on and had his harness fitted securely. The helicopter was now ready for immediate takeoff.

J.J. clicked another remote on his set of keys. Above the 109, the roof split into two halves and within minutes, the roof was completely open to the elements. The same engineer who had designed the opening roof of Wimbledon had worked on James's electronic roof. £10K cash on top of his invoice had ensured his silence. When they clicked open, J.J. carefully raised the collective lever to bring the chopper into the black sky. He turned the engine power control slightly, and the Augusta 109, very quickly, was flying at 1000 feet and was several miles away from the coastline where his derelict building had the automatic roof slowly closing.

J.J. flew low over the English Channel and joined the purple corridor on sight of land. This was an exclusive section of airspace which is reserved only for any royal flights. Through his father's royal connections, J.J.'s G.P.S. always kept him flying directly on track. Any air traffic controller looking at his screen at that time of night would assume the flight had royal connections and wouldn't expect any radio contact. J.J. flew directly north, and five miles before Sandringham Castle, J.J. veered over the wash and flew at zero feet directly eastwards across the channel to a landing site north of Amsterdam.

In a deserted spot, a lorry flashing his lights guided J.J. to a place to land. Very quickly, two things would happen. Three men would approach the 109E where Boz stood at the opened cargo door to supervise the loading and unloading of the cargo J.J. had flown to this deserted area. Two of the three men were armed with repeating rifles for protection in case the operation was discovered by the Interpol drug squad. Boz and J.J. were armed in case the customers tried to take the load from the helicopter without paying. Both parties were hoping that this was going to be a lucrative and long-term partnership, so there was a certain amount of trust between them.

One of the men checked what J.J. had brought, and Boz checked what was given in exchange. Within minutes of landing, they both took off, bringing the 109E Augusta to a five foot hover. Slowly turning around, J.J. flew off westwards into the distance.

J.J. was happy with his cargo hold full of heroin, and the lorry drivers were more than happy with their one million euros in used fifty euro notes.

No one, but no one, had seen a thing.

It wasn't until the next night that J.J. got the text on his phone that gave him the G.P.S. co-ordinates where to drop his load off. Once again, Boz and he travelled to the field where the helicopter was, this time by a different route. After only 10 minutes flying, they came across quite a large grand house with gardens to the front and, conveniently, a tennis court which had its net taken away and all six floodlights turned on for J.J. to safely land the 109E. J.J. had been instructed to stay in the helicopter whilst two men disguised in balaclavas unloaded the heroin. So, that was the first delivery complete.

A really nice way to earn five grand, thought J.J.

As he flew back to the helicopter's hanger, J.J. thought about the risks he was taking. He wasn't that bothered about his father's new agent. He didn't come across as the type. He actually came across as quite a nice bloke. There was no way he would find out about any of J.J.'s illicit trading, and there was no way he would discover the Augusta 109E as he only flew at night. It, once again, would be so easy that if he got too close to Scott Parker's operation, or even was close to finding out about J.J.'s new venture, this latest agent would be dealt with the same way as his father before him. He would have an unfortunate accident.

Chapter Sixteen

The Hospital Visit

Queen Elizabeth Hospital, just south of the River Thames in London, is the largest hospital in London. To give you an example of how busy they are, they handle 5000 telephone calls a day. The intensive care unit was right at the top of the building so that, when they brought Mark in by helicopter from the scene of the car crash, he was able to be taken straight into the I.C.U. ward where specialist doctors were on hand to treat him immediately.

Jack felt guilty about not visiting his brother, Mark, in hospital as much as should have. His mum and Susan were there constantly, wiping the sweat off Mark's brow, even shaving his stubble every couple of days.

Jack always sat holding Mark's hand when he visited him, but there was never any response. The doctors couldn't tell the family how long Mark would be in a coma and if he ever would come out of it. Jack often thought about what Michael Schumacher's family must be going through as, after his skiing accident, Schumacher was still in a coma even after several years. Jack would often glance at Mark's life support machine. It was the only thing that was keeping Mark alive. Jack dreaded being the one responsible for switching it off if it ever came to that.

Jack was in the M.I.5 building just north of the River Thames only a couple of miles away from the hospital waiting for his next assignment. He had a couple of hours before he was due to be picked up, so he decided to walk across the bridge and spend some time at the hospital to give his mum and sister a well-earned break.

Jack sat with Mark, holding his hand, and telling him about the time they both climbed the tallest tree in the woods near where they lived and Mark fell and broke his leg. Jack laughed when he recalled Mark's nickname was Peg Leg as Mark had to wear a calliper for six months and was unable to catch Jack after Jack had shouted out Peg Leg and ran safely away from his hobbling brother. After six months of healing, both legs were strong again but one leg was an inch shorter than the other. Mark would always walk with a slight limp.

Jack was brought out of his daydream when Mark's hand started to shake. At first, it was only a slight shake, but it got so bad Jack called out to the nurse. It was the staff sister who responded and told Jack it was common in coma patients. As the shaking continued, the sister said that Mark was only dreaming, and it was a good sign that his brain was starting to respond to Jack's touch. Little did they know that Mark wasn't dreaming — he was having a nightmare!!

Chapter Seventeen

The Car Crash

It was all supposed to go smoothly. A 'doddle' was how it was described to Mark at the meeting with his father, Commander James, and another young, recently trained operative, Steve Gibson. The department had received intel that a new crack house was operating selling drugs in South London in one of the tower blocks that dominated the skyline. Mark Senior was to drive his son and Steve to the tower block and wait outside while the two young lads went and bought some drugs.

They were to act naive and innocent asking questions like, "What sort of drugs do you sell?" and "How much are they as we only have one hundred pounds each to spend?" They had to find out as much information as they could. Both lads had dressed in what they thought was appropriate for the world of drug culture. Both wore jeans and white trainers. Mark wore a bright blue hoodie, and Steve wore a bright orange hoodie. Mark explained to his dad that they were gang colours.

Mark Senior took an old Toyota Corolla out of the carpool so as to fit in with the area. It would be no good at all to take one of the souped-up M3 B.M.W.'s.

Mark Junior and Steve arrived at the tower block. Mark Senior stayed in the car whilst Mark

Junior and Steve set off. After the Grenfell disaster, all the tower blocks had been stripped of their cladding to give the area more of a look of East Germany before the Berlin Wall came down.
As usual, the lifts had been vandalised, so the boys had to climb 48 sets of stairs to get to the top.

"Leave all the talking to me," said Mark as he knocked on a solid iron door. The small square shutter at eye level was drawn back.

"What d'ya want?" said a black face.

"Hi," said Mark. "My name's Shorty Smith and this is Macca McClean. The landlord of our local pub told us we could score some gear here." The shutter was closed only to be opened a couple of minutes later by a white face.

"Stand clear of the door with your hands behind your heads. I don't know you guys so no funny business."

"O.K. O.K." said Mark. He and Steve did what they were told to do as the big iron door was slowly opened.

"Have you got any weapons on you?" growled White Face.

"No," replied both Mark and Steve together.

Black Face appeared and said, "Turn around, hands held high, while I search you both. You can never be too careful."

Black Face searched Mark first, a thorough frisking including turning out his pockets.

"How much money's in there?" he asked looking at Mark's wallet.

"A hundred pounds," replied Mark.

"Well that ain't gonna buy you much. We only deal in crack cocaine, heroin, L.S.D., etc. None of your soft drugs like Ecstasy tablets. They're only for the kids." He laughed as he started to search Steve. "What the hell's this?" he said as he held up Steve's British Intelligence I.D. card. "Your name's not McClean, it says here your name's Steve Gibson."

"They're the bloody filth!" he shouted. No one was more shocked than Mark. How the hell could Steve make such a basic mistake to bring his real I.D.? Mark couldn't believe what happened next. There was a tussle and both men grabbed Steve and threw him over the wall to his death! There wasn't even a scream. Mark reacted by attacking Black Face but only managed to hold him in a sort of bear hug. To his horror, White Face pulled a gun out and raised it. Mark recognised the gun as a Glock 17. Lethal at such a short range. Before the gun was fired, Mark managed to turn Black Face around. There was the crash of the 9mm bullet being fired and then the sound of the bullet disintegrating Black Face's spine. Before White Face could shoot again, Mark threw Black Face's body at White Face, bowling the man over. This gave Mark a chance to escape. He ran down the stairs faster than he had ever run.

A second bullet smashed into the concrete of the final stairwell, covering Mark with dust and confirming White Face was close behind.

Mark Senior had heard the gun shots and drove up onto the path to the entrance of the tower block.

He had no time to check the bright orange hoodie that indicated it was Steve's body. It had landed grotesquely onto the top of an old Ford Cortina caving the car's roof in and setting off its alarm.

Mark ran over to the Corolla, opened the passenger door, and shouted, "Go! Go! Go!"

Mark Senior revved the Corolla engine to the max and, with screeching tyres, headed out to the main dual carriageway road quickly establishing that White Face was in hot pursuit in a black Lexus. Mark Junior breathlessly explained what had happened.

"What a cock up. The Lexus is gaining on us, and I assume he is still armed." Mark's father was concentrating on his driving, repeatedly glancing in his rear view mirror to check the progress of the following Lexus. It only seemed like seconds before the Lexus drew level with its passenger window already down. White Face was driving with his left hand whilst aiming his gun with his right. Mark's dad swerved and rammed the Lexus. White Face struggled to drive the Lexus and aim the gun at the same time. Only seconds later, the two cars were neck and neck.

"Get down!" shouted his dad.

As Mark bent down, he heard the explosion of the gun going off. His father's warning had saved

Mark's life but not his own. The bullet had hit his father's neck and passed right through his throat and then carried on to smash the passenger window on the Corolla.

In a rage, Mark grabbed the steering wheel and lunged the Corolla into the Lexus once again. Above the screeching of high speed metal on metal, Mark could hear a screaming voice. It was his own. Mark's dad's body was leaning onto the steering wheel making it difficult to steer.

The two cars were locked together going faster and faster as Mark's dad's foot was wedged on the throttle of the Corolla. They were approaching a tunnel. Mark gave the Toyota one more desperate turn into the Lexus. The two cars separated.

The Lexus swerved onto the opposite lane, narrowly missing a black cab. The Lexus hit a retaining concrete wall which launched the car into the air at 90 miles an hour. It flew like a missile away from the road and rolled down an embankment. It settled at the bottom of a gorge. Amidst the carnage of the smoke and wreckage, a white arm could be seen trying desperately trying to open the driver's door to escape. A massive explosion followed by a raging fire ensued. White Face would never sell any more drugs.

The Toyota was massively out of control. It mounted the pavement and ran straight into a road sign advising drivers to switch on their headlights for the approaching tunnel. The car never reached the tunnel as it went from 90 miles an hour to zero in a millisecond. The seat belts and air bags might have saved Mark from serious injury if it wasn't for the pole of the sign ending up halfway inside the engine block and landing on Mark's head with a sickening thud.

Jack was still holding Mark's hand as the shaking subsided. He was still completely unaware of the real truth of his father's death.

Chapter Eighteen

The Concert

Jack left the hospital and returned to the MI5 building as he had to get changed for his next assignment. He was to attend the Royal Albert Hall for a concert starring Holly Anne Parker. After taking a shower, the dresser who was responsible for all of the agents clothes, cars etc. dressed Jack in a black evening suit with white tie. Black patent shoes finished off the look. The dresser then gave Jack the keys to a white Range Rover Sports and told him he had to be at the Royal Albert Hall box office at 7 pm to pick up his ticket. Jack parked his car about a mile from the venue and walked the rest of the way.

He was soon joined by a throng of people all dressed in evening dress for the concert. Jack picked up his ticket. Second row from the front, very impressive. He entered the auditorium and was surprised at how big it was. He sat down and stared at the stage which had only a white grand piano, a set of drums, and a bass guitar and amp. The venue was filling up quite nicely when a group arrived to take up the whole of the front row. Jack recognised Scott Parker from the intel photographs, his wife, and his son John. Jack assumed the rest of the front row was Scott's guests. He was surprised to see J.J. amongst the guests.

Jack managed to catch his eye and gave him a quizzical look as if to say, "What are you doing here?" J.J. just smiled and looked away. There was a warm round of applause as a young lady and two musicians took to the stage. They went straight in and played three back-to-back jazz classics from Miles Davis, Charlie Parker, and John Coltrane. This was met by an appreciative round of applause. Jack didn't clap his hands. He just stared transfixed at the beauty of Holly Anne. He had never seen a more beautiful girl in his life and wasn't aware there was an interval until most of the front row got up and went to the bar to partake of their reserved drinks.

J.J. sat alone. Jack took advantage of the opportunity to lean over and speak to him. When asked what was he doing there, he replied that he was a friend of John Parker, Holly Anne's brother. They had gone to Eton together and had stayed in touch.

"Do you want me to get you an invite to the after concert party? It's at one of Scott's clubs, The Rooftop Gardens."

"That would be brilliant," replied Jack as the front row started to fill up for the second half. Holly Anne came onto the stage alone. For the first half an hour of the second half she played selections of Mozart, Beethoven, and Chopin. You could hear a pin drop. Holly Anne seemed to gel with the piano and the audience to create a magical atmosphere that had the audience on its feet when she took her first bow.

She then went back on the piano, and for the first time, spoke to the audience whilst the drummer and bass player took up their positions. She thanked her family and especially her parents for all that they had done for her. Both Scott Parker and his wife stood and turned to acknowledge the applause. For the rest of the concert, she played modern classics from the catalogue of Elton John, Michael Buble, and Billy Joel. She even did an incredible jazz version of Elvis Presley's 'Are you Lonesome Tonight'.

By the time the concert had finished and Holly had taken half a dozen curtain calls, Jack was totally besotted by her. He'd never felt like this about a woman. He looked upon his current girlfriend Louise more as a mate than anything else, and to his complete surprise at the after concert gig, he was standing with a glass of champagne in his hand when he heard a voice from behind.

"Well, did you enjoy the concert?"

Jack turned around and blurted out that he had enjoyed it very much.

Holly replied, "Well, I just had to meet the young man who couldn't keep his eyes off me all night." Holly gave a lovely laugh whilst Jack went crimson with embarrassment. Holly walked on to mingle with the other guests. Jack was gutted.

Chapter Nineteen

The Holiday

The next morning Jack attended the debrief with Commander James.

"Did you see any proof regarding his other business?"

Jack replied, "Nothing at all. Scott Parker and his family just come across as very successful. They're very popular with all the right people. There were two M.P.'s at the party. One who is in the cabinet. A Radio 1 D.J. was playing the dance music, and the catering came direct from Harrods. The food and champagne were excellent. The Cristal Champagne comes in at £150 a bottle, and they were glugging it back like there was no tomorrow."

"Well, Jack," said the commander, "you have to get a lot closer to the family. Find out more about his nightclubs. His national security company. His drugs suppliers. The man must make a mistake sometime. The whole family is off on holiday to a place called La Manga in Spain. Very upmarket. They have rented a penthouse apartment. I have booked you and your sister into the apartment below. There will be a full surveillance team in the apartment opposite with full view of the penthouse and the communal swimming pool that they will be using. Try your best to get in with them. Your cover story is that you are a professional disc jockey, and you are so glad you met him, as you've always wanted to work in one of his nightclubs."

Jack couldn't believe what he was hearing. He'd never D.J'd in his life. Hosting a family karaoke party was about his limit.

"What if my sister, Susan, doesn't want to get involved?"

"Just tell her you need her help to track down the criminals who were responsible for your father's death."

Surprisingly, Susan was up for it. She wanted to help and admitted she needed a holiday from visiting the hospital twice a day.

Jack didn't sleep at all that night. How was he going to approach Scott Parker with the unlikely tale that he was looking for a gig at one of his nightclubs? What were the chances of Jack ending up being on holiday at the same apartment block as the Parker family? He decided to ring Commander James in the morning as Jack was puzzled that Commander James's only son J.J. was part of Scott Parker's entourage. Why couldn't J.J. try to get the information about Scott Parker's other activities? Commander James was not pleased when Jack rang him. He explained that his son wasn't a trained undercover agent, J.J. was a really good friend of Scott Parker's son, and that was the only connection. He wasn't prepared to risk J.J.'s life.

However, Jack could say that J.J. had chatted to him at the concert, told him about how fabulous

La Manga was as a holiday resort, and why didn't he try and get a last minute deal and join them. This made meeting up with the Parker family a much more likely scenario, and indeed, it happened at Murcia International Airport as they were waiting for their bags at the carousel. Jack and Susan had flown Ryan Air from East Midlands. The Parker entourage had flown first class with British Airways from Heathrow. It was lucky that both flights had arrived within minutes of each other.

"Hi, we meet again." Jack turned around only to be faced, once again, with the beauty that was Holly Anne Parker. He quickly introduced Susan and explained that he knew J.J. who had recommended La Manga for a holiday, and they were very pleased to get a last minute deal on the apartment below them.

"Great," said Holly, turning to Susan, "Perhaps we'll meet up later for a drink around the pool."

"That would great," said Jack. He enjoyed the view as Holly walked off.

"She's nice," said Susan. How was Jack supposed to reply to that?

Jack couldn't stop thinking about the situation. He was infatuated with the daughter of the man he might have to end up assassinating. Jack suddenly felt he was in over his head and dreaded lying to a girl he was besotted with and also lying to a girl back home he no longer cared for.

Chapter Twenty

The First Contact

Scott Parker was well-pleased with his decision to come on holiday. He had definitely been working too hard lately, and it would mean a welcome break for himself and his family. Lying by the pool, hiding behind his sunglasses, he was able to think things over.

All four of his nightclubs were doing good business as well as the little side-lines he had going. J.J. and his side kick Boz were doing well keeping control of the stock of drugs and the cash they generated, and he wasn't due to go out to Thailand until Xmas. So, the supply of cocaine from his contact in Phuket was arriving on time at the end of each month, regular as clockwork. He transferred the funds required from his Swiss bank account, but he was aware that it made good business sense to keep the supplier sweet by visiting him every three months just in case there were any small problems or niggles that needed to be discussed.

Now, what about the problem of this so-called agent J.J. was telling him about? He had reminded him of the old saying, "Keep your friends close but your enemies closer."

Surely that didn't mean inviting them to come on holiday with them! Scott didn't agree in the decision to allow the man and his sister to come to

La Manga. What was he going to do? Arrest Scott? He was just going to follow J.J.'s advice: be friendly and just enjoy your holiday.

The first morning of their holiday, Susan and Jack decided to spend some time lazing around the communal pool. It was over 30 degrees centigrade, so a quick swim and some sunbathing was the order of the day.

They had both attended a briefing with the guys in the opposite apartment block who would be videoing and recording everything in the hope that Scott or a member of his family would talk about their drug operation to give the bosses back home something to go on.

Both Scott and Susan were discreetly wired up to record any conversations they might have with the Parker family.

The surveillance team had already put hidden microphones and cameras inside Scott's penthouse apartment. Within a day, they were in luck. Scott received a phone call with the international code for Amsterdam from a guy who had a holiday villa in the village of Los Nietos, near La Manga. He was coming out tomorrow, so perhaps they could meet up for a drink to discuss business.

The only person Scott and Susan spoke to on their first day was Holly Parker. This suited Jack, although he was conscious that he was beginning to behave like a love-struck teenager whenever Holly was about.

When Holly removed her bikini top to do some topless sunbathing, Jack was quite beside himself and purposely buried his head in his Kindle trying to concentrate on his book.

"We're all going to Dante's tonight for an Italian meal. Do you guys want to join us?"

"That'll be great," said Susan. "What time?"

"See you there about 8pm," said Holly who put her top back on and went back into her apartment.

Jack was in luck that night. He was sat next to Holly, and although he thought she was teasing him half the time, they got on really well, and the evening was a great success.

As the evening came to a close, Holly bent over and whispered to Jack.

"Meet me at the pool later for a midnight swim." They both giggled like a couple of teenagers. Scott spotted this and responded by leaning across the table to speak to Jack.

"What do you do young man?"

Jack, keeping up the pretence of his cover, replied, "I'm a professional entertainer, disc jockey and karaoke presenter, sir."

"No need to call me sir, son. Scott will do nicely."

So that's his cover, is it? He'll be asking for a job in one of my nightclubs next, thought Scott. *Christ! British intelligence is a joke. I bet they've got cameras all over the place. I'd better watch what I say*, he thought.

When the evening finished and the bill was presented, Scott paid with his card.

"How much do I owe you, Scott, for Susan and myself?" asked Jack.

"No problem," said Scott. "It's been a good week."

Jack will never know how good, thought Scott to himself.

The next day, Jack was in the surveillance apartment when a black Mercedes turned into the car park and two men got out. Both wore dark suits despite the high temperature, and dark glasses added to the rather sinister look. They both went into Scott's apartment block and took the lift up to his penthouse. Jack watched as the surveillance engineer switched channels on his recording equipment so as to record all of the men. Unfortunately, they held their meeting on the rooftop terrace outside the scope of the microphones and cameras, so they were unable to record anything of importance.

A couple of times voices were raised, "You've got no freaking chance!" was one of the lines shouted out, but the others weren't so clear.

Scott wasn't happy with how the meeting was going. He had J.J. and Boz there as security in case things turned a bit nasty. He'd been doing business with these guys for almost three years with no problems. They supplied the amount of Ecstasy tablets required, and Scott transferred the funds, no problem.

Their argument was the kids of today were smoking more marijuana which was leading them onto harder drugs like crack cocaine and heroin. They were finding it difficult to supply the amount of Ecstasy tablets that Scott's nightclubs needed every week. Would Scott consider going into the harder drug market?

So, this was the crux of the matter. It was all bollocks about having a limited supply of Ecstasy tablets. These guys just wanted to switch markets to hard drugs for more money.

Scott was beginning to lose his temper. Were these guys trying to have him over? Obviously, the harder drugs were more lucrative, but Scott was old school; he just saw Ecstasy and cocaine as fun drugs, something to help the night go better and longer. He didn't fancy his punters starting to overdose in his toilets with needles stuck in their arms which would bring in the police straight away to investigate his businesses.

The dealers suggested changing the terms of their deal. They would have to put their prices up.

That was when Scott shouted, "You've got no freaking chance!"

The dealers then turned and went. "We'll be in touch," was their parting comment.

Scott nodded to J.J. who in turn nodded to Boz. Boz fully understood. The two guys were to be taken out.

Boz waited until nightfall before he went out to the pool. Making sure there was no one about, he unscrewed the four screws that kept the cover on the air conditioning unit. He reached in and pulled out a long leather case. He then walked swiftly up the steps away from the communal pool, opened the driver's door of the small seat hire car, and drove away. It was only minutes later when he was on the motorway heading to the first junction which led to the village of Los Nietos.

J.J. had given Boz directions, so he knew the Armenians' villa was the last one on the left. He drove past it and didn't stop until he had driven some 400 yards into the Spanish bushland. After parking the car, he spent quite some time to find the best advantage point overlooking the pool of the villa, which was his target. Now it was just a matter of waiting.

Boz thought back to the first time he had killed a man. He was 10 years old. It was at the height of the Serbian Croatian war in the 1990s in which 140,000 citizens were killed. He had just returned from school and was upstairs getting changed when all he heard was shouts and screams. The shouts were from his father and were swiftly silenced by the rattle of an AK7 automatic machine gun. Boz dashed downstairs only to see his mother bent over the kitchen table whilst a Serbian soldier was thrusting his body into hers. Boz grabbed the soldier's pistol, removed it from its holster, and whilst the solder turned to look at him in surprise, Boz quickly shot him in his face. The soldier's head exploded, and Boz's mother slid, sobbing, down to the floor.

Boz never knew what the soldier was doing to his mother until, as a boy soldier at the age of 15 fighting in the war, he saw his own comrades do the same to young Serbian girls. Such were the horrors that he experienced, and Boz soon became hardened to it all. So, it wasn't a problem when several hours later, after waiting patiently for the sun to come out and the two Armenians were relaxing by the pool, that Boz lay down to assume the traditional sniper's position.

His weapon of choice was the American Rifle M24 S.W.S. (Sniper Weapons System).

Supremely accurate for up to a mile, Boz was confident it would only need two shots to take the two Armenians out.

Although he was over 400 yards away, he could clearly hear the sound of conversation and the high pitched giggles of the two prostitutes that had been hired for the night who were enjoying themselves at the pool.

Conditions were perfect. The blazing sun was coming up to full temperature as Boz wiped his forehead for the last time before he gently squeezed the trigger.

The first guy just gently fell off the small diving board he had been sitting on. The only sound was the splash of the water as he fell in. One of the girls, who was in the water, laughed as she thought she was being dive-bombed. It was only when the water around the shape at the bottom of the pool went dark red did she realise something was wrong. Her screams towards the other guy to catch his attention only succeeded in the guy lifting his head from the book he was reading. Both of the girls were now looking at him to do something when the front of his face just disappeared in a mist of blood. There was no sound from the M24 as the silencer Boz had fitted was the very latest attachment to the weapons system available for the rifle. Both girls gathered up their clothes and, screaming, went inside the villa to get away from what was obviously a sniper.

Boz wasn't bothered about the girls phoning the police. What were they going to tell them? They hadn't seen him, so there was no chance of a good description being given. His only problem now was to go back to the villa, then wait until it was dark and replace the M24 in its hiding place, making sure no-one could see him doing it.

The La Manga police report a few days later was brief and to the point. Two men had been shot and killed whilst relaxing next to their pool in their holiday villa in Los Nietos. The men had long been suspected of criminal dealings in the UK. The police concluded that it was a professional killing.

Scott was pissed off. Now he had to go to Amsterdam and find some new suppliers.

Chapter Twenty-One

Midnight Swim

Jack was at the pool early. He had told the surveillance team what was happening. They were excited that, at last, Holly might just let slip what her father really does for a living.

Jack had contacted the commander back at MI5's headquarters to give his daily report. He could tell Commander James was extremely unhappy there was nothing to tell him. Jack wasn't bothered one bit. He was just looking forward to having some alone time with Holly.

Jack was sitting on one of the pool's sun beds when he looked up as Holly approached. She was wearing a long white beach towel around her neck and nothing else. Jack was gobsmacked!

"Let's leave the swim until afterwards."

With that she pushed Jack back onto the sun bed. She removed the towel to reveal her stunning breasts and mounted Jack.

Jack arched his body and removed his swimming trunks to release his excited penis which Holly, rather expertly, inserted into her very welcoming vagina.

Holly rocked back and forth, her moans a clear sign of her pleasure. Her rocking movement started off slowly and gently increased. Jack thought his body would explode, and it took all of his willpower to restrain himself. When both of their worlds climaxed, Holly's body collapsed onto Jack's, and they both lay there for several minutes enjoying the age-old glow of contentment.

"Are you O.K.?" Jack inquired.

"Yes," replied Holly. "That was lovely."

They lay there for a few more minutes.

Jack started thinking about his girlfriend Louise. His pang of conscience didn't last very long as Holly made to leave.

"What about our midnight swim?"

"We'll do it tomorrow night, Jack, goodnight."

Jack just lay back on the sun bed. The guys in the tech apartment weren't going to be very happy at what they had recorded that night. Jack was no nearer to discover what Scott did for a living, and, more to the point, he had no valid evidence to put forward to the commander. Jack couldn't see just yet if there was enough reason for Commander James to want Scott assassinated. He would just have to get a job in one of Scott's nightclubs to see if he could dig deeper into Scott's operations. Jack knew the final decision of what was to be done lay entirely with him. All he knew was Scott just came over as a successful businessman, and Jack was falling in love with his daughter. This could, if he wasn't too careful, turn into a right mess.

Chapter Twenty-Two

Amsterdam

'Big Chris' Van Dijk had been dealing in drugs ever since he took over his dad's flower business. Chris was a mountain of a man. Six foot seven in his stocking feet, his fellow employees were astounded that a man with hands as big as shovels could take hold of a bunch of roses, thorns and all, and create a beautiful bouquet in less than a minute. The only thing that impressed Chris was the fact that he had just turned five euros into fifty. So, from the money from his flower business and drug manufacturing, Chris was doing very well, thank you.

Based in the small village of Haarlem just outside Amsterdam, it was ideal. Some 30 miles from Schiphol Airport, the farm was on the outside of the village based at the end of a dirt track so they wouldn't be bothered by anyone, including the local police. Although he grew a substantial amount of flowers all the year round, the busy times, i.e. Easter, Xmas, etc. he would import what was needed from Holland. The flower business was made better by the small chemical laboratory further up the dirt track where two highly paid chemists manufactured Ecstasy tablets. The drugs policy in Amsterdam was very unusual. You could buy marijuana in any of the cafes. Four joints could be bought for the price of a packet of cigarettes and, strangely enough, you could carry on your person up to five Ecstasy tablets for personal use.

Anywhere else outside of the city you were only allowed one tablet! Taking advantage of very little interference from the local police, Chris was able to supply most of the city's cafes with their Ecstasy needs although it was dealing with the English markets where Chris made the big money.

One of his best contacts was with two Armenian guys, Davit and Alex Grigoryan, who seemed to have most of the English accounts sown up. After a period of dealing with cash, Chris now had his payment paid directly into his bank account on a standing order. It was that simple. One or two meetings a year was all it took to keep the supply flowing when the amounts may be had to be changed a little.

Davit and Alex had not been around for a while. Chris wasn't too bothered as he hadn't heard there was a problem, so he just manufactured as normal. Everything was going well until one day, he noticed a strange car driving down the dirt track. He had to duck under the doorway of his office as he stepped outside. The car obviously wasn't going to the farm, as he wasn't slowing down. Chris just managed to stand in the middle of the road to wave the car to stop.

"Hello, is there something I can help you with?"

"Are you Chris Van Dijk?" asked the visitor in a rather thick heavy English accent.

"I'm here on behalf of the Grigoryan brothers."

"Sure, come in. I've just made a pot of tea."

The stranger followed Chris into his office.

"My name is Navik Grigoryan. I am their eldest brother. I am here to tell you my brothers have been murdered."

Chris nearly dropped the teapot as he was pouring out the tea. It was plain by Big Chris's reaction that the news was a complete shock to him.

"Would you, by any chance, know anything about it?"

"I haven't seen them in a while. I just assumed everything was going as normal," replied Chris.

Navik leant forward to pick up his teacup. As he did so, his jacket flapped open to reveal a holster with a Luger pistol in clear view. This definitely concerned Chris.

"I need to know the details of your customers as I am convinced it would be one of them who actioned the assassination."

"Haven't you got the details on computer?"

"Yes, but, unfortunately, I cannot access the accounts as I don't have the password. My part in the company is security. I am responsible for the safety of the Kardashian family, which, as you might suspect, is a full-time job. So, in future, you will be dealing with me when I take over the drugs side of our business until I can find someone who I can trust to deal with you."

Chris sat with his head in his hands.

"Wait a minute. I have some old files where the addresses are kept of our original customers. They are mostly details of the many cafes we supply, though there are the details of our first English customer, the Parker family, who not only operate four nightclubs in England, they too have security connections and supply concerts, football matches, and other large events. They also deal in cocaine, which I think they most probably source in Thailand as we only deal with Ecstasy. Is that of any help?"

Chris passed the files to Navik who bowed his head in thanks.

"The last phone call from my brothers told me they were going to see Scott Parker to try and persuade him to start dealing in heroin. If he wasn't too keen, they were just going to have to raise the prices on the current deal on the supply of Ecstasy tablets. I'll have to track Mr. Parker down and ask him a few questions. Just keep producing your tablets as ordered. I will let you know if there is any change in quantity."

As Chris waved goodbye to the departing car, he sighed with relief. He wouldn't want to get on the wrong side of Navik or any of his associates. Perhaps he should retire from the drugs business and concentrate on flowers. Selling roses wouldn't get him killed.

Chapter Twenty-Three

The Break-Up

Jack was feeling great after his holiday at La Manga Club. He also felt a little guilty. He was supposed to gather evidence against Scott Parker's drug empire but, fortunately for him, all he did was fall in love with his daughter, Holly, and spend several nights indulging in lovemaking by the pool followed by a midnight swim.

Jack had caught the train down to London to attend the debrief in front of Commander James and the surveillance crew.

"Nothing on tape we could use then?" asked the commander. The crew as one shook their heads.

"What about you, Jack? I hear you spent quite a bit of time with his daughter, any joy?"

Jack obviously couldn't tell him there had been a lot of joy but not of the right kind.

"The whole family seemed to be there just to enjoy their holiday. Your son, James, was there. Did he not mention anything?"

Commander James was clearly annoyed that Jack was now asking the questions.

Jack quickly followed up his question by saying, "James had a mate with him. A Croatian going by the name of Boz. I have no idea what his role was. He never said much. I don't know if he was some kind of bodyguard. It might be worth the tech guys investigating him."

"Well, if that's all we've got, let's investigate this character called Boz. I always thought he was a friend of James and was there to drive James about whenever required.

"Delve into his background. It might give us a couple of leads we can follow."

Just as they were all leaving the room, Commander James added, "By the way, there were two Armenians murdered at their villa in Los Nietos a few miles from La Manga Club whilst you were all there enjoying your holiday. Let's investigate that. You never know, there might be a connection to the Parker family."

Jack decided to get the train to Oxford and spend the night with Louise. They had spoken a couple of times on the phone but the conversations were shorter than usual. Jack had decided to break up with Louise as all he could think of was Holly Parker. Although they had made no plans to meet up, Jack was convinced Holly was the one. He had no idea where it would all lead to especially if it was decided that her dad was to be taken out.

Louise seemed genuinely pleased to see Jack when he arrived at her flat. She had bought herself a puppy. A white standard poodle who was all over Jack after he had sat down. Jack was pleased as they both loved animals. Jack had felt guilty that his dog had spent more time in kennels lately with everything that was happening in his life.

Louise made them both pizza and it was afterwards, after coffee, that Jack broached the subject of their relationship.

"I need to talk to you about us."

The opening line could have been worded better as it immediately killed the atmosphere.

"What do you mean?" asked Louise who was already starting to get upset.

"My job seems to be taking me all over at the moment. I've just come back from Spain, and there's talk of a long-term surveillance job, so I will have no idea when I'll have the time to see you."

There was silence. Jack couldn't think of saying anything else as he had a feeling he would just start telling lies.

"You know I can't say too much because of my job, but I think we should spend some time apart so we can both concentrate on our careers."

"Is that what you truly want?"

"I think it's for the best."

With that, Louise got up and went into her bedroom, slamming the door shut behind her.

Jack spent an uncomfortable night on the sofa being constantly woke up by the poodle licking his face. He finally gave up, pulled on his joggers, and walked to the railway station to get the early train back to Market Harborough.

Chapter Twenty-Four

Amsterdam Re-visited

Scott had a meeting with J.J. and Boz as soon as they all had got back from Spain.

"I need you to get cover for our deliveries over the next couple of days. We have no big events this week and the clubs are quiet mid-week, so there should be enough stock to do us until the weekend."

"What have you got planned?" asked Boz.

"Obviously, with the Grigoryan brothers out of the way, it gives us an opportunity to find the manufacturer and deal direct. We'll have more control over our supplies and, as we are dealing direct, there will be a saving which will give us more net profit. I have booked us on the early shuttle to Amsterdam in the morning. If we are lucky and we find our new supplier, we can get the evening flight back."

"What about weapons?" asked J.J.

"I don't fancy going into the unknown without being tooled up. There's no chance of us getting our revolvers through English customs."

"OK, then," replied Scott. "Whilst we are asking around about where to find a supplier of Ecstasy tablets, we can discreetly enquire about the availability of firearms."

It was the first time Scott had been to Amsterdam. J.J. had been on a couple of stag weekends where the rest of the lads had taken full advantage of the red light district which had left J.J. feeling non-plussed.

It was on their visit to a third cafe where they struck gold. The owner was the cousin of Big Chris Van Dijk who, not only being the biggest supplier of flowers in the city, also had a rather lucrative side-line supplying all the cafes with their Ecstasy needs.

Scott expressed his thanks with a handful of euros. He felt comfortable enough then to ask about weapons.

"The police, if they stop you, won't prosecute you if you have drugs on you for personal use, but if you are found to have weapons on you, you'll be arrested and banged up for a couple of months. These guys have zero tolerance on guns of any description. You won't have any problems with Big Chris. He's a gentle giant."

Scott thanked him. No weapons of choice for Boz. On the way back to their hire car, Scott couldn't stop Boz from going into a hardware shop and buying the biggest knife that they sold.

"I feel a lot more comfortable now I have this in case anything does kick off."

Following the cafe owner's directions, they found themselves driving down the dirt track leading to the large greenhouses in the distance that housed Chris's flower business. The car they had hired at the airport was finding the dirt track a bit rough but eventually stopped when a really large bloke stepped out and waved them down.

"Hi, are you Big Chris? Your cousin told us where to find you."

"What do you want?" Chris was being deliberately naive as he didn't know these guys from Adam.

"Well, let's just put it this way. We're not here to buy flowers. My name is Scott Parker, and you have been delivering our orders for several years now through a third party. The third party has now gone out of business, and I'm here today to negotiate a deal to buy direct from you."

"So, what's with the other two guys?" asked Chris as he bent down to clock Boz and J.J.

"I brought them along as I thought I might come up against some resistance to my plan, but so far, I've been impressed by everyone's pleasant attitude. Can we come inside to talk business?"

Chris motioned to them to come into his office. He wasn't totally unaware of the irony of the situation. One day he is giving Navik Scott Parker's address details, a few days later he meets the man himself. For the moment, he wasn't sure how he was going to play this.

"Let me start by saying I want to be completely straight with you. I have fallen out with the Grigoryan family as they wanted me to start dealing in heroin. When I refused, they threatened me with a price rise for my Ecstasy tablets. I only allow Ecstasy and cocaine into my outlets. I don't want the horrors of my customers becoming heroin addicts which inevitably will lead to police involvement. As of now, I have had very little police interruption. I see the fire service and the guys from the local council health and safety departments more than I see any police. So, I would like to deal with you in the future. I will split my additional profit 50/50 with you as a gesture of good faith."

The thought of additional profit perked Chris's ears up, but he suspected that Parker wasn't aware of the third brother who was currently trying to track him down to have what Navik called loosely further negotiations.

"Well, I am certainly interested in your proposal, but I feel I must wait for a while to see if anyone from the Grigoryan family contacts me about continuing our present arrangement. Would that be acceptable to you and your colleagues?"

Scott could see the sense in what Chris was proposing. He was sure that Chris had no idea about what had happened to the Grigoryan brothers, so he didn't mind waiting. He now had Chris's website details and said he would e-mail Chris in a few days to see what the situation was. He was a bit puzzled when Chris mentioned other members of the Grigoryan family. As far as he knew, there were only the two brothers.

Ah well, if there was any trouble coming from that direction, Boz would just have to deal with them. Scott was determined to have full control of his supply with no middle-men to deal with. It worked a treat in Thailand where the producers of cocaine dealt with him directly, and he had had no problems whatsoever. Scott hoped that in the future, when things had settled down, it would be the same as his Ecstasy business.

After they had shook hands all-round, the three of them drove back to the airport well-pleased with the day's work. There might have been a more sombre atmosphere on their journey back if they knew Navik had booked himself into a small hotel opposite to Scott's The Rooftop Gardens in London and had settled in patiently waiting for their return.

Chapter Twenty-Five

Scott's First Kill

Navik Grigoryan was sitting inside by the bay window in his hotel on the ground floor with a clear view of the entrance of the The Rooftop Gardens London nightclub on the opposite side of the road. He had already spent several hours during the day, but with no movement, as the nightclub didn't open during the day, he was expecting better luck during the evening.

For the umpteenth time, he checked the safety latch was on and the Walther P38 revolver was fully loaded with eight 9x19mm parabellum cartridges. He would have preferred to have brought his Luger into England, but the tight security at the airports meant he had to make a quick visit to one of the cousins, Bruno, in the east end to secure the loan of the Walther.

With only a range of 50 metres, it meant that Navik had to get up close to Parker to ensure accuracy, and that meant getting into his nightclub so he could, hopefully, make his way upstairs to the Parker family flat. He was hoping Parker would be alone with the family residing in their family home in Leicestershire. The apartment was only used when Parker needed to stay over when he had business in London. It was about 10 o'clock when Scott arrived. He got out of his Rolls Royce and went inside. One of his door staff took the keys and drove off to go behind the building where there was a small car park for Scott and his senior staff. Navik clutched his pistol in anticipation.

Scott went upstairs to his apartment. He sat looking out at the view of London at night and tried to think things over. He was beginning to think killing the brothers had been a mistake. He had made the decision when he was angry. He should have waited until the next day when he had calmed down. He had certainly raised the stakes of his involvement in the world of drugs. He knew there would be repercussions. He had taken to carrying his small derringer pistol in the sock on his right foot. He had to be ready for anything. J.J. had wanted to stay in London with Boz, as bodyguards, but Scott preferred Boz to go back to the Midlands to protect his family with J.J. going back to his own house to wait for further instructions.

Getting into the nightclub was easy. Navik wasn't even searched. He just paid the 10 pounds admission and made straight for the bar to order a pint of lager. He sat on a bar stool. There was only background music being played as it wasn't at all busy. There were very few customers to bother the two barmaids. Navik sat and observed. He could see a sign for the toilets, and as he made his way over, he spotted another door marked 'Private'. This was obviously the staircase up to the living quarters. After staying in the toilets for a few minutes, he quickly came out and tried the door marked

'Private'. It was open. With a glance over to the doorman, who was too busy chatting, he opened the door and swiftly closed it behind him. He stood inside the small entrance and waited to see if anyone came. After a few minutes, he quietly made his way upstairs and trod carefully as not to make a sound.

Scott had already received the text from his head doorman confirming there was a customer, who looked remarkably like the brothers in the photograph, who had just entered the club. The staff was instructed not to approach the man as he was to be considered highly dangerous. Scott looked down on his phone to see he had another text saying the man had entered the door marked 'Private' and was on his way up the stairs to the private accommodation. Scott opened the glass door that led onto the outside Juliet balcony of the apartment and pressed his body close to the wall. He heard the apartment door being swiftly opened by Navik, and Scott held his breath.

For a couple of minutes, Scott heard nothing. Navik was next door searching the master bedroom and en-suite. Then the sound of desk doors being opened and rummaged in could be heard through the glass door, and, for one moment, Scott hoped that Navik would just go assuming the apartment was empty.

This was not to be, as the glass door opened. Navik stepped out, gun raised, and looked to his left. It was when he looked to the right and saw

Scott, he hesitated for that fatal second. Scott already had his derringer pistol raised. He fired one shot into Navik's forehead. Navik immediately slid to the ground. Death was instantaneous.

Scott dragged the body back into the apartment. Looking down, he could see there was very little blood. There was no exit wound at the back of the head. The small pistol had just enough power to be fatal at close range. The bullet was obviously still inside Navik's head. Scott went into the bedroom to get a couple of bed sheets to wrap the body in. Now, what next? How the hell was Scott going to get rid of the body?

He decided to sleep on it. He would come up with a plan in the morning. He felt less guilty now about killing the elder brother after authorising the assassination of the two younger brothers. If he hadn't have done so, Scott was convinced they would have taken over the drug, and most lucrative, side of his business.

Scott picked up Navik's gun. He recognised the make and model. A Walther P38 loaded with parabellum bullets that would have blown Scott completely off the balcony if Navik had been just the one second quicker in firing it. Scott unloaded the clip containing eight 9mm parabellum cartridges. He sat on his office chair. The adrenaline was still coursing its way around Scott's body, and as he held the pistol in his hand, he could see he was shaking. He then remembered the meaning of the word parabellum. It was Latin for 'If You Seek Peace Prepare For War'.

Chapter Twenty-Six

The Crematorium

Scott Parker was sitting in his Rolls Royce Phantom with a dead body in the boot. He had parked in the customer car park of the Cransley Gardens Crematorium near to his flat in Wimbledon. There must be money in dead bodies as there was an additional building recently added on to give the discerning member of the grieving family a choice of the original 50-seater or, if the deceased had been really popular, they could be booked into the 100-seater.

Simon had been to a few funerals in his time, and he was convinced, for a lot of people, it was just a good excuse for a piss up and a day off work. It had become that bad in his nightclub business he had recently made a rule if you wanted a day off to go to a funeral, it came off your holiday entitlement.

Scott waited for the last group of mourners to head off to their reception. Even then he had a good look around to make sure there was no staff, gardeners, etc. He then drove around to the side of the building where the office entrance was. Just as he got out of his car, the funeral director was at the door locking up.

He noticed Scott, turned, and said, "Can I help you with something?"

"Yes, I would like to book a funeral."

"Is it possible for you to come back tomorrow and see my secretary? She works nine to five and will give you all the details you require."

The funeral director turned to lock the door, so he didn't initially see the Glock 17 9mm pistol being taken out of Scott's shoulder holster. When he did turn around, all he could do was cough and splutter at the site of the gun barrel pointing directly at his chest.

"We need to talk, bud. Just unlock the door. I'll try and not take up too much of your time."

The door was swiftly opened, and Scott was led into the admin office.

"Sit down and listen very carefully. I have a dead body in the car, and this is what you are going to do."

The funeral director's name was Wayne Johnson, 31 years old, a thin slight build of a man, married with two daughters. Wayne was unable to speak as he was in a state of shock.

Scott carried on. "Here are a couple of photographs. You'll see that they are of your two daughters, Polly and Hannah, ages 5 and 7. The other photograph is of a zebra crossing. This is the crossing where your two daughters cross over at roughly 8.45am every day on their way to school. If you don't agree to cremate the body I have in my boot, I will arrange to have both of your daughters run over in a hit and run accident. The car used will have false plates and will not be traceable. Do you understand what I am saying?"

Wayne could only nod. He couldn't believe this was happening.

Scott then removed a jiffy bag type of envelope from the inside pocket of his suit.

"You normally charge between 2-4 grand for a routing funeral. Inside this envelope there is £5000 cash. Once again, if you do not deposit this money into your personal bank account, I will make the call about your daughters. You are well aware that cremating bodies unofficially will render you a rather long jail sentence. Try explaining to the police that you weren't in on it with £5K in your personal bank account.

"We will do the cremation now and an hour from now you will be on your way home with £5 grand in your pocket with no one the wiser as I am definitely not going to contact the police, and you are now well aware of what will happen if you have a pang of conscience, are we clear?"

Wayne just nodded like a puppy dog. There was one small part of him thinking about what holiday he could book for his family with the cash he was given.

He couldn't believe he was helping to lift a body bag from the boot of the Rolls Royce. He thought it best not to speak as he was well aware the man had a gun, and Wayne assumed he had used it before. Most probably on the body he was about to cremate.

Scott stood by as he watched the body bag move slowly towards the incinerators. It was unusual not to see an expensive ornate coffin. Instead, it was just a black plastic zipped up body bag carrying the Serb who had tried to kill him. Scott was pleased that there would be no trace of the body and when he got his next visit from the boys from Amsterdam, which would surely happen, he could deny all knowledge of ever meeting his assailant.

Chapter Twenty-Seven

Jack Needs A Job

The decision to have the second de-brief meeting after the uneventful trip to La Manga Spain in the MI5 building was a mistake. Commander James was grossly unhappy that a surveillance trip which had cost the British taxpayers close on £100K had resulted in absolutely nothing. His raised voice could be heard throughout the corridors of power, and it wasn't like him to use language normally associated with building labourers.

"Now I've just heard from our boys in Intel that Parker is taking his wife on holiday to Phuket in Thailand. He's just come back from a frigging holiday! You'll just have to get a job in one of Parker's nightclubs. He already thinks you're a disc jockey of some repute."

Jones was standing now pointing his finger directly at Jack. "Make sure you get a job here in London at The Rooftop Gardens. I don't want him sending you to some God forsaken town north of Glasgow."

"What if he wants me to audition? I have very limited experience playing music and working a dance floor. He's bound to spot it. What if I just ask for a job behind the bar? At least I can do that. I worked in several bars to earn money to put me through my three-year degree course."

"Do what you bloody well think will get you inside his organization. Use that girlfriend of yours, Holly, is it? She can wield her influence with her father to get you a job.

"Just get enough evidence that Parker is an international drug dealer and, using his contacts, arranged to have your father killed, and just remember, your brother is still hospitalised lying in a coma. When you've got enough evidence, you know what you have to do."

With that, Commander James left the room and, to show his displeasure, slammed the door shut behind him.

It was quite easy for Jack to ask Holly if she could put a word in with her father about a bar job. He just said it was embarrassing that when they had arranged to meet up and go out for a meal after coming back from Spain, Jack didn't have enough money to pay for the meal. Holly just laughed and paid the bill with her debit card.

"Dad will give you a job. I got the impression he quite likes having you around. My brother John has gone back to work in the city, and I'm off on tour next month. Are you sure you don't want to come with me? You could be my roadie."

Jack was stuck for words as he couldn't tell Holly about his brother, Mark, who was lying, still seriously ill, in St. Thomas's hospital. There was no way he could leave him for any length of time.

After leaving the meeting with Commander James, Jack decided he would go home and try and get some rest to give him a couple of days to think things through. Whilst walking to the station, his phone went off indicating he had a message.

"Jack, Jack, please pick up. Come to the hospital as quick as you can. Mark's awake, Mark's awake!"

Jack couldn't believe what he had just heard. If Mark recovered, it would be a bloody miracle. What if he did fully recover?

Perhaps he could help Jack sort out the Parker situation. Things were getting more confused day by day. As far as Jack could see, Scott Parker was just a businessman who dealt in soft drugs as a profitable side-line. If Jack arrested him on that charge, and it being Parker's first offence, it would be surprising if the judge would give Scott a custodial sentence. The Parker family wasn't doing anything that would warrant Jack killing anybody. Jack was a million miles away from learning who killed his dad. Could it have been Scott Parker? Jack's relationship with Holly didn't help. Jack was falling in love with her. He knew he shouldn't mix business with pleasure, but he was completely besotted with her. Hopefully, Mark could now shed some light on their father's murderer.

When Jack arrived at Mark's room in the hospital, he was met by his mum and his sister both hugging him and shedding tears of relief. Mark was sitting up in bed with tubes up his nose, his chest and head heavily bandaged, but, when he saw Jack, he was able to give him a weak smile.

Jack held his hand and felt stupid when all he could say was, "How are you feeling, big brother?"

"I've had better days," replied Mark.

Jack pulled up an extra chair so he could sit by Mark's bedside holding his hand. Susan and their mum sat the other side of the bed.

"I've already told Mark about our trip to Spain, but, unfortunately, he cannot remember anything before his 21st birthday."

"You were helping Dad on a drugs case, Mark. Don't you remember anything?"

"I can remember how hard my training was and how proud Mum was at my passing out parade. After that, nothing."

"You can't remember Commander James, our boss?"

"What do you mean our boss?"

"I have agreed to join the Special Services in order to find out who Dad's killers were."

"You have joined us. What about your flying career?"

"That's just a thing of the past now, Mark. You don't remember having a meeting with Commander James or the mission that you were on with Dad?"

"I'm sorry, Jack. Everything's a blank. My doctor has suggested that with complete rest my memory might improve little by little."

Jack looked up at his mum. "How much do you know about what I'm involved with at the moment?"

"Susan has told me everything. I'm so worried, Jack. I thought I was about to lose one son. I don't want to lose another."

Jack could see Mark was getting tired.

"I'll leave you now, big brother. You get some rest, and I'll be back tomorrow. I'll go through everything with you then: my training and my efforts up to now in trying to find Dad's killers. Perhaps I'll be able to jog your memory somehow."

With that, Jack left and made his way to St. Pancras to get the train home to Market Harborough. He didn't sleep that well that night. He just lay there hoping Mark could remember the nightmares he was having whilst he was asleep. Jack was convinced if they could unlock the memories, that would help Jack unravel the facts of the case, and they could come to a conclusion that would satisfy Commander James.

Chapter Twenty-Eight

The Tsunami Nightmare

Scott Parker couldn't sleep. The thought of three deaths being attributed to him was keeping him awake most nights. He didn't know what to do next. He had e-mailed Big Chris in Amsterdam saying he hadn't heard anything from the Grigoryan family so could they trade direct? Big Chris gave Scott the new price. They split the extra profit 50/50, and everything would carry on as normal.

Although he wasn't due to go out to Thailand for another month, Scott decided he would go early. Maybe the trip would do him good, and he could put these nightmares behind him. He even thought of taking his wife, Harriet, with him this time. She had never been to Phuket in Thailand before, and Scott knew that she would love it. It might help get their relationship back on track as Scott, to be frank, was getting fed up with his hectic lifestyle and was keen to get back to normal married life. He obviously wouldn't be introducing Harriet to any of his business partners, and he would tell his two girlfriends over there to keep a low profile because, this time, he was going to be bringing his wife.

Scott lay in bed and thought back to his first trip to Phuket and the horrors of the tsunami. There were nearly 200,000 reported deaths when the Indian Ocean earthquake had caused the tsunami to hit. Scott was upstairs in his hotel room with the girl he was involved with then when it happened. A beautiful Thai girl called Achara lay beside him. Achara was Thai for pretty angel, so Scott always called her that. His pretty angel.

It was the day after Xmas day and about nine o'clock in the morning. Scott and Achara were awoken by a shuddering of their building as though they were having an earthquake. It wasn't too serious, but it was enough to awaken them. Scott had had a really rough night. It had been a brilliant Xmas day celebration. Glen, an Australian and also the hotel owner, had put on an all you can eat Thai buffet and Scott and Achara had exchanged presents. Thailand didn't celebrate Xmas, but Glen was determined to put on a special day for his English guests. Scott felt a little bit guilty on the phone wishing John, Holly, and Harriet 'Merry Xmas', but they knew he was in Thailand for business.

What they didn't know Scott always seemed to mix business with pleasure. Achara had gone to bed, and Scott had got involved in a card game with Glen and two of the other hotel guests, and the game, with the drinking, went on until the very early hours. When Scott announced he was going to bed, Glen and the other two guys said they were going to take a walk down to the beach and have a nightcap at their favourite beach bar. The hotel was only a small building. It was built over the car park on the ground floor and then two further floors with

10 rooms on each. Scott always stayed in the top floor as he always loved looking at the sea view. Achara said she was going to work that morning as she had a few bookings booked into the massage parlour.

Boxing day was just like any other day to Achara, being Buddhist. She was in business with her sister, and Scott had generously put up the money for the business, and he was pleased with the look, complete with lovely white leather chairs and massage beds that he had helped Achara design. The massage parlour was based on the beach at the sea front along with other businesses: bars, restaurants, etc. as far as the eye could see. The beachfront bay was very popular with tourists, so it was always packed.

The atmosphere was brilliant as music would be playing from the various hotels that were situated in the second line behind the hundreds of businesses on the front line. The first thing Scott knew about the tsunami was the roar of water that was approaching his hotel. The hotel was half a mile from the beach, so how come he was hearing rushing water? He quickly got out of bed and went to the window, only to see an image he would never forget. There was a wave of water coming towards him carrying along with upturned cars, remains of buildings, ripped up trees, and, what was most horrific, hundreds and hundreds of bodies. If it hadn't been for the underground car park, Glen's hotel would have been washed away. Fortunately, the bulk of the water just went through the ground floor. It took all of the cars with it including Scott's Toyota Landcruiser. The hotel was built on concrete stilts which were strong enough to withstand the onrush of millions of gallons of water.

There was nothing Scott could do but to wait until the tsunami had settled down with most of the sea water retreating back to the sea, leaving behind an unbelievable sight of carnage and floating bodies.

It was late in the day before the sea had finally settled although the police weren't allowing anybody near the sea front.

The next morning, Scott went downstairs. There was no sign of Glen or the other guests. A police car was patrolling asking people who had survived to go down to the beach and give blood at a makeshift hospital that had been set up in the local primary school which, thank God, as it was a Saturday when the tsunami hit, had been empty of children.

Scott walked down the road that normally led to the beach. This time, though, he had to pick his way through the destruction. It came as no surprise when he saw one of his white leather chairs hanging from the remains of a tree. Scott waited at the end of a queue that seemed to go for at least a mile to the hospital. Four hours later, after he had given blood, he walked along the water edge trying to see if Achara's body was amongst the hundreds still floating in the sea. Most had distended stomachs as the gas in their bodies bloated and expanded all of their limbs. It was a horrific site. There was no sign of her. No sign of her business. All of the businesses along the water's edge were makeshift affairs. They had all been destroyed. Hundreds of bars, restaurants, parlours, etc. had just disappeared. Scott was determined to do something to help. He stayed a week longer to set up his foundation that would provide food and shelter initially, and, hopefully, when things got back to normal, his plan was to provide enough money to give the children a smart school uniform and at least one hot meal a day.

He was pleased he was going to invite Harriet on his next trip. He would be proud to show her what the Parker Family Foundation had created in the schools of Phuket.

Chapter Twenty-Nine

The Family Cousin

Bruno Grigoryan was getting worried. It had been a week since his cousin Navik had paid him a visit and asked him to lend him a gun. Bruno had made sure he was always sufficiently 'tooled up' as he was having trouble with some Kosovans who were trying to hone-in on his territory. Bruno's main business was trafficking. It was fairly simple to go back home and approach good-looking young girls that he could give a job to in the U.K. where they could learn English and, generally, make a much better life for themselves.

In reality, it was completely different. They were made to live in a room sharing with three other girls, and most evenings they were transported to houses where there was a crowd of men drinking and having a party. The girls were expected to join in and make full use of the upstairs bedrooms whenever they were told to do so. They were only given one meal a day. The only luxury was Bruno always made sure his girls were made up and were always dressed in the skimpiest of dresses when they were working. When the girls got home at night, they were made to strip and put their old and bedraggled tracksuits back on. One or two of the girls had tried to escape. The first one was beaten so badly she had to walk with a stick. The second girl who tried it disappeared. It was rumoured she was murdered, cut up, and fed to the fishes in the nearby River Thames.

Bruno tried ringing Navik's phone for the umpteenth time. No answer, straight to voicemail as usual. It was time for him to do something. Navik had told him that he was having trouble with a nightclub owner who Bruno suspected had had his two younger brothers murdered. Bruno could understand why the nightclub owner had reacted in the way he did. The two men should have been content with dealing in Ecstasy tablets and not try to force a deal which included heroin. Bruno decided to visit the nightclub with three of his workforce. He went to his locked cabinet that he kept his armoury in. When he opened the door, there was a space where the Walther was usually kept. Alongside it were two S.A. 80 assault rifles and two light machine guns. More than enough for the job in hand.

Chapter Thirty

Jack's New Bar Job

Jack was enjoying his new job. Holly had asked her dad, and Scott seemed very keen for Jack to join the company.

"That lad's got a big future ahead of him," was Scott's response to Holly's request. Jack started work the following Monday. He already knew how to pull a pint and serve customers from his student days of part-time work, but he had to learn all the different cocktails that were on the menu, and also he was trained in how to change a barrel down in the cellar.

He enjoyed the bookwork side of the business, how to check in deliveries, and also make sure the tills were correct at the end of a shift. Even though the majority of trade was with contactless debit cards, there was still a fair amount of cash to worry about. He was even trusted to go to the bank to deposit takings and buy any change that was needed for the weekend.

Luckily enough, Jack was down in the cellar the night of the attack. After hearing the unmistakable sound of gunfire, he initially thought he should go upstairs, but his revolver was in his bedroom at his flat. Jack didn't think it would be needed when he was working at the club. How wrong can you get?

Bruno and his three accomplices just drove up to the front door of the nightclub just after opening at 10 o'clock. The car screeched to a halt and a few seconds later, all four men, complete with black balaclavas to cover their faces, rushed the door. Bruno had given strict orders that no-one was to be killed. It was an easy matter to knock both doormen out with the butt of their rifles.

On entering the nightclub, Bruno shouted at the two bar staff, "Get down and lie on the floor."

All four men then proceeded to spray the nightclub with rifle bullets and the destructive force of the light machine guns. It was absolute havoc. Jack was down in the cellar and had locked himself into a room that kept all the wines and spirits, hoping the upstairs gunmen wouldn't come there. Bruno detached himself from the other three and broke down the door to the upstairs flat, hoping to find Scott Parker. He took his frustration out on the empty flat by destroying all the furniture and fixtures with repeated bursts from his light machine gun. Firing 300 bullets a minute, it didn't take Bruno long to completely destroy everything.

The attack only lasted a matter of minutes before all four men made their getaway in the black Mercedes with false number plates on.

Jack emerged from the cellar to find the two barmaids crying hysterically and the two doormen leaning against the bar both bleeding heavily from head wounds. Jack immediately called 999 for an ambulance. He had no idea what to tell the police as they would undoubtedly follow the ambulance to the club. Jack recognised immediately that the attack had raised the stakes of his investigation to a much higher level. What the hell had the Parker family done to constitute such a violent reaction?

Chapter Thirty-One

Decisions

Commander James had called an emergency meeting after hearing reports about the shootings at the nightclub.

"Had you any idea it was going to happen, Jack?"

"No, sir," Jack replied. "Although I'd only been working there a couple of weeks, I'd seen no sign of drug dealing. The first suspects are usually the doormen. They both came across as really nice blokes who concentrated on getting on with the customers rather than just being there to throw people out."

"What about Parker, any sign of him or his family?"

"Parker has a flat there, as you know, but all the time I've worked there, I've seen no sign of him, his wife, or his son and daughter. I just assumed he and his wife were still on holiday in Thailand, his daughter is on tour, as you know, and the son, John, I don't think is involved in any way shape or form in the family business."

"What's your thoughts on the attack?"

"Well, sir, I think it must be connected to the Spanish murders. No way were the two brothers in business with Parker by themselves. There must have been others involved, possibly family members, who wanted to take revenge. Judging by the weapons they used, we're not dealing with amateurs."

"We'll just have to see how Parker reacts when he comes home. I'm going to put more men on surveillance duty. I think he needs to be watched 24/7. Apart from the drugs issue, I don't want a full-blown gang war on our hands. We've got to nip it in the bud as soon as possible. What's your position in the club now?"

"I've just been told to stay at home and wait until the repairs are done and the club is ready to open. I think with the amount of damage done, it'll be at least a couple of weeks."

"One good thing is we've had the report back about Boz. Apparently he's ex-army, no previous form, seems he started off as a doorman and now does work for my son, James. So, I don't see any problem there. I think we can discount him."

The meeting broke up with Commander Jones saying that Jack should take the opportunity to have a couple of rest days, maybe visit his brother to see if there is any progress in his recovery.

Chapter Thirty-Two

Jack Makes A Discovery

Jack woke up the following morning after his meeting with Commander James, determined to take a couple of days off. The shootings in the nightclub had shaken him more than he would like to admit. He now carried his Glock 19 pistol with him wherever he went. He wasn't prepared to take any chances.

With luck, Holly had a couple of days free from her touring schedule, and Jack had tickets for her final show before the break at the nearby Derngate Theatre in Northampton. He was to meet her after the show and then take her back to Middleton to spend a couple of days together.

Jack's mum and sister, now that Mark was recovering, had moved back into their home, so it was with great pleasure that Jack introduced his mum to Holly. It was obvious that they would get on as his mum gave her a nice welcoming hug and immediately offered her the obligatory cup of tea. Susan had got on well with Holly in Spain, and soon, they were chatting how was the tour going, etc. Jack had already primed both his mother and Susan not to mention anything about what Jack really did for a living.

He had decided to surprise Holly the next morning. So, after making her breakfast, they went off in his dad's Lexus to an unknown destination. Holly laughed with pleasure when, after driving some 20 miles, Jack turned off into Sywell Aerodrome and parked next to his Cessna two-seater aeroplane with the registration number GO-JAK printed on both sides of the fuselage.

Holly had never flown in a light aircraft before and was very excited about it.

"Where are we going today?" she asked.

"I'm taking you to Le Touquet in France for lunch."

"Wow!" said Holly. "Will it take long to get there?"

"We'll be making a short trip down to the coast to Lydd Airport at Romney Marsh. We need to land there to pass through customs and file a flight plan so they know where we're going and what time we will be expected back. I'll also use the opportunity to fill up with fuel so we will have enough for the flight there and back home to Sywell."

Conditions for flying were perfect. Although Jack had filed his flight plan into the aeroplane's computer, there was no need. Cruising at 3000 feet, he could see clearly where he was going, and very soon the small airport appeared on the horizon.

"Why don't you go to the restaurant and grab a coffee whilst I go to the control tower and book in?"

The afternoon went really well. Jack had organised a driver to pick them up at Le Touquet

Airport. Although there was only one runway there, it was still quite busy as it accepted international travel as well as light aircraft.

After a superb lunch, the car took them back to the airport and, after doing all the necessary checks, they were soon landing at Lydd Airport.

"I won't bother with a coffee whilst you are booking out this time. I'll just nip to the loo."

Jack walked over to the control tower, and Holly made her way to the Ladies. As she was entering the toilets, she caught a glimpse of a man leaving the Gents. She was sure she recognised him but just couldn't remember where from.

"All set?" said Jack as he leant across and tightened Holly's seatbelt.

"Do you know I've just seen someone coming out of the toilet. It took me a couple of minutes to think about it, but I'm sure it's that chap that hangs around with J.J."

"Boz! Are you sure?" asked Jack.

"I'm not that sure. If it isn't him, it's his twin brother."

"Wait a minute," said Jack. "I'll go back to the tower and check who else has flown in and out today."

After climbing the stairs to the tower and explaining to the controller he had to check his entry as he thought he had made a mistake, Jack opened the booking-in book and scrolled down the entries. There was nothing on the first page but, after turning the page over, he couldn't believe the

164

first entry on the previous page. There it was in black ink handwriting, James James. Jack moved his finger across the entry to see what aircraft was booked in.

"Bloody hell," he exclaimed. "He's flying an Augusta 109E Helicopter." What the hell was J.J. doing down at Lydd Airport flying a quarter of a million pound helicopter and with Boz in the passenger seat?!

Jack went back to the Cessna deep in thought. There wasn't a lot of conversation flying back as it was getting dark, and Jack needed to concentrate on his flying skills.

Where was J.J. flying off to? It couldn't be that far as he would have to fly in the dark. Commander Jones had ordered extra surveillance teams watching Scott Parker 24/7, but what about watching J.J. and Boz? Jack always followed his gut, and his gut was telling him J.J. was up to no good.

****

The next morning Jack drove Holly to Leicester for the next stage of her tour at the De Montfort Hall. All of Holly's gigs had been sold out in advance, and there was talk of a television show at the end of the tour. They were now firmly seen as a couple, and Holly had already asked Jack about moving in with her after the tour. Jack felt he was stuck between a rock and a hard place. He just couldn't see himself living in the same house as a man he might have to kill.

With Scott Parker still on holiday in Phuket, Jack now made it his mission to find out about J.J. and his movements. The world of private helicopter owners in England was a close-knit one, and Jack felt it wouldn't be too difficult to find out where J.J. kept his helicopter and, on top of that, find out the flight details to see what he was up to flying at night.

Jack drove directly from Leicester to Sywell to see if he could find out anything. Michael Thomas was the guy in charge of servicing the aeroplanes and helicopters that flew in for their regular 50 hour check, aviation's answer to a M.O.T. Luckily enough, Michael was in his office next to the service hangar when Jack drove up.

"Hi, are you here to fly the Spitz today?" he asked.

"Nah! No more stunt flying for me at the moment, Michael, busy doing other things."

"I know I haven't seen you for a while. Can I just say, I was so sorry to hear about your dad, Jack? He was a cracking bloke."

"Talking about my dad, Michael, he left me quite a bit on money, and I'm thinking about buying a helicopter. I've seen an Augusta flying in and out of Sywell a few times. What do you think about them?"

"Well, you are talking top drawer there, Jack. A quarter of a million pounds of anyone's money, but it's a beautiful thing to fly. You're in luck. We have one in the service bay getting its 50 hour check. I'm sure the owner wouldn't mind me showing you around it."

Michael spent the best part of an hour showing Jack around the machine that belonged to J.J.: the benefits of a jet engine as opposed to an ordinary petrol engine and the luxury of autopilot where the machine just flew itself. Jack was getting impatient. He didn't want to be there if J.J. turned up. Too much of a coincidence. All Jack wanted to do was to get inside the 'copter.

"Do you think the owner would mind if I had a sit in, just to get a feel of it?"

"I'm sure that would fine."

Jack sat in the cockpit pretending to take in the cluster of instruments on the dashboard when all he was really doing was finding the ideal spot under the pilot's seat where he could place a magnetic tracking device. The hi-tech people at MI5 had given Jack the aviation answer to 'find a phone'. J.J. wouldn't be able to go anywhere now without Jack knowing. What Jack did notice was the trip details on the machine's computer. It stated the machine had flown a distance of 38 miles from where it was based. Jack had just assumed the machine was kept at the big house on the coast where J.J. lived. That trip was certainly more than 38 miles. Jack would love to know where the helicopter was kept.

"I'd better go now, Jack, as the owner is expected quite soon, and I have to sort out the paperwork and invoice for work done."

Jack bade Michael farewell and thanked him for his time. When he got back into the Lexus, he checked on his Apple smart phone that the app indicated the Augusta was stationary at Sywell.

He decided instead of going home he was going to get the Cessna ready for immediate take off and, with the help of the app, he could follow the Augusta and find out where the helicopter was based.

It was about an hour later when Jack saw the mechanics wield the Augusta out onto the taxi-way. Minutes later, J.J. got into the pilot's seat followed by Boz in the passenger seat. Whatever anyone thought about J.J. and his lifestyle, they couldn't argue about his flying skills. He brought the machine to a five foot hover, executed a complete 360 degrees to check if there was any other traffic in the circuit, and flew off heading southwest.

Jack was now able to ask the tower for clearance to take off and, using the app, was able to follow the Augusta. He had already done all the pre-flight checks that were necessary, and with full power, the Cessna soon reached its take-off speed of 60 knots. Jack actually preferred flying at night because all the towns were brightly lit up, and he knew straight away he had got Northampton on the nose, and 1000 feet below he could the flashing green and red warning lights of the Augusta. They had only been flying for 20 minutes or so when Jack could see from the app the helicopter was descending.

Jack dropped the power from the Cessna's engine and followed suit. Jack was quick to spot a bright light suddenly appearing in front of the helicopter, and as Jack flew closer, he was amazed to see the helicopter was indeed landing in its hanger, but this time, he was descending down through an open roof! As Jack flew over the hangar, he could see the roof closing on itself, and within minutes, there was complete darkness.

As Jack flew back to Sywell, he was well pleased he had accomplished the first part of his mission. He now knew where the machine was held. All he had to do was to find out where J.J. was flying to in the dead of night.

Chapter Thirty-Three

Jack Meets Big Chris

Jack didn't have too long to wait to find out where J.J. flew at night. The alarm on the 'Find A Target' app on his smart phone woke him up at two o'clock in the morning.

Jack watched the tracking device which indicated J.J. was flying east.

Jack went downstairs, made himself a cup of coffee, and watched the app on his phone.

An hour later, the blue line on the phone stopped. Jack could see the final destination was somewhere in Holland. Jack's fingers touched the screen on the phone to enlarge the image, and he could see the helicopter had landed somewhere west of Haarlem which itself was only 20 kilometres west from Schiphol Airport in Amsterdam.

Jack went back to bed to try and get some more sleep as it was his intention to fly to Schiphol in the Cessna, hire a car, and then drive to the point where the Augusta had landed.

He was up early the next morning and decided first thing not to take his Glock pistol. He couldn't risk customs discovering it, and possessing a gun wouldn't fit well with his cover of just being an interested tourist.

There were no hitches for Jack when he flew, once again, down to Lydd, then crossed the channel, and was soon given permission for finals to land from the air traffic controller at Schiphol Airport.

So it was just after 10 in the morning when Jack pointed the nose of his hired Toyota down a dusty dirt track which, as far as he could see, led to row after row of greenhouses.

From what he could see, the greenhouses were just growing large numbers of flowers. Nothing suspicious so far.

A quarter of a mile later, he could see he was coming to what seemed to be the reception office of what appeared to be a wholesale flower business. He was flagged down by a giant of a man. Jack looked at his phone and could see he was at least a mile from where the helicopter had landed during the night.

"How can I help you, sir?" Big Chris's English was good but spoken with a heavy Dutch accent.

"I'm looking to buy some flowers." Jack knew at once his answer was very weak. "I own some hotels in England, and I thought whilst I was in Holland, I might procure a trade deal for quite a substantial amount of flowers that I use for my reception desks, our wedding and meeting rooms, and also the rooms themselves." Jack was just thinking on his feet.

"Do you not think that after packing the flowers and then flying them to England would first of all increase their price and, more importantly, shorten the lifespan of whatever you buy? Surely it would be cheaper to buy them locally, and the flowers would last longer."

Jack knew he was getting nowhere.

"Ah! Well, thanks for your help. Can I turn around at the end of this track?"

"You can turn around here. Just make a three point turn."

Jack got the distinct impression that the big man did not want Jack to drive any further down the track.

"Cheers then, thanks for your help."

Jack drove back to the airport hotel where he booked in, parked the car, and went to the airport restaurant to buy some lunch and to formulate a plan going forward.

Jack waited an hour after sunset, got into the Toyota, and drove 20 kilometres to the point where the dirt track started just off the main road. Jack hid the car in a field just after the start of the dirt track and headed off on foot to see if he could find anything that would explain the helicopter landing here in the middle of the night.

Jack followed the dirt track until he spotted a small path that led to the greenhouses. Using his torchlight app. on his phone, he ascertained that the first row of greenhouses did indeed grow flowers. The next row, because of that unmistakeable smell, were growing marijuana plants, and the final row were growing poppies. Jack had found a commercial operation whose cover was the growing of flowers but also dealt in the manufacturing of marijuana and heroin. Jack decided to look further on past the reception area. After a half of a mile, Jack came to another smaller building. This was where the app. showed the point where the helicopter landed. It was easy to break the lock on the door of the building and, pointing his torch, he could see what were big jars used for cooking. Was this the operation that manufactured Ecstasy tablets?

Two things then happened simultaneously: the building was flooded with light from dozens of overhead L.E.D.'s, and a voice boomed.

"Once again, is there anything I can help you with?"

Jack turned to be faced with the giant of a man for the second time that day.

Big Chris just walked up to Jack and punched him full in the face. One punch was all that was needed to render Jack unconscious.

It was light when Jack started to come round. Apart from his head pounding with pain, Jack soon asserted he was sitting on a metal chair with his legs and arms bound with plastic garden ties. He was in the building with all the cooking pots surrounding him.

"My name is Chris, also known as Big Chris, for obvious reasons. What the hell are you doing sniffing around my business?"

Jack didn't really know how to play it.

"I know the laws in Holland are fairly lax when it comes to personal use of drugs. You can hardly say that this operation is for personal use, can you?"

"There is a huge demand for marijuana and Ecstasy tablets in Amsterdam. I'm just meeting a demand. Strictly business."

"That's fair enough, I suppose, but what about the poppy fields? Are the laws relating to heroin the same?"

Big Chris laughed. "You could say I am meeting demand from other countries."

"Is that where the helicopter comes in?"

Big Chris moved forwards raising his hand to strike Jack once again.

"How in the hell do you know about helicopters?"

"It's just a wild guess," Jack lied, feeling the blood running down from his bottom lip. "I shouldn't think you would use boats when the English Channel is full of patrol boats nowadays looking out for rubber dinghy's full of immigrants."

"You've certainly got a point there. For your information, I have put a call into the organisation that I deal with so they can tell me exactly what I'm going to do with you. So, for the time being, stay where you are. If you try to escape, I will have to shoot you. Do you understand?"

Jack could only nod his head and to try and prepare himself for a long period of time sitting in this chair with the plastic ties cutting into his flesh.

Chapter Thirty-Four

Holly is told The Truth

Holly was standing in the middle of the stage with arms outstretched, acknowledging the applause of over 5000 people who had paid strong money to attend her last concert of the tour at the Royal Albert Hall in London.

She motioned her bass player and drummer to join her at the front of the stage so all three could bend and shake hands with the audience who were crowding around not wanting the excitement of the concert to end.

After a few minutes, all three left the stage for the final time, waving farewell as they went.

Sitting alone in her dressing room, Holly was overcome with the emotion she always felt after a successful concert. She was obviously very pleased at how the tour had gone, and the prospect of a T.V. special was very exciting for her, but she hadn't heard from Jack for two days, and he always called at 6 pm before she went on stage but, despite numerous messages left, she still hadn't heard from him. She was looking forward to having some time off at her parents' home in Rutland and was hoping Jack could join her there. The only time her mum and dad had met Jack was in Spain, but she was hoping that after spending some time with them as a family, they might grow to like him and see that their relationship was a serious one.

The next morning, she decided to phone Sywell Aerodrome to see if she could ascertain whether the Cessna was parked up or if had Jack flown off somewhere.

It was the chief engineer, Michael Thomas, who answered the phone, and when Holly asked about Jack's whereabouts, he could only tell her that Jack had filed a flight plan to Amsterdam with no details, as yet, about a return flight.

"So he must still be in Amsterdam then?"

"It looks that way," replied Michael. "Have you tried phoning him?"

"I left message after message. I'm afraid there might be something wrong. You hear about light aircraft going down in the English Channel all of the time."

"Don't you worry about Jack. He's too good a pilot for that to happen."

It was with heavy heart that Holly boarded the train to take her up north.

Her mum and dad had come home early the day before from their holiday in Thailand after hearing about the attack on their London club, so Scott was available to pick her up from the station and soon commented about how quiet she seemed to be.

Was she pleased how the tour went? Was she happy about the forthcoming television special?

One word replies only indicated to Scott that there was something wrong. Was it her love life?

"Are you and Jack still an item? Your mother and I haven't heard a lot about him lately. I thought he was coming to stay for a couple of days?"

"So did I," replied Holly. "I haven't heard from him, and there's been no replies to the voice mail messages I have left him."

The rest of the car journey home was done in silence. When they arrived, Holly went into the house as Scott put the car in the garage. Even Harriet noticed that Holly was quieter than usual.

When Scott came into the house, she turned to him and enquired, "What's wrong with Holly?"

"Jack hasn't been in touch. Apparently, he's in Amsterdam. What he's doing there is anyone's guess."

Scott decided to take the bull by the horns in regard to the relationship between Holly and Jack, so he decided to tell her some of the truth concerning what Jack really did for a living.

Scott finished his meal, put his knife and fork down, and pushed his chair back, turning to Holly so he could speak directly to her.

"Holly, you know what happened at the London club, don't you?"

"Yes, you said it was between rival drug gangs fighting over some sort of turf war. I know the club hasn't been reopened yet because of all the damage done, so why hasn't Jack got in contact as

177

he most certainly won't be working at the club until the reopening, will he?"

"No, he won't be working at the club at all."

"Why not?" enquired Holly.

"We've heard through our sources that Jack has already got a full-time job."

"What's that then? Why hasn't he told me?"

"You have to prepare yourself for a shock. Jack is an MI5 agent working to try and track down the suppliers of the drug trade in London."

"You must be joking! Jack's a lovely guy. He wouldn't be involved in anything like that. Anyway you have always maintained that the drug problem happens well away from any of our clubs, so how is our family involved? Does Jack think we are a family of drug lords?"

Scott now had to be careful at how much he could tell his daughter. There was no way she could find out about how Scott ran his other business. All Scott did was to find the feeder pub that most of his customers met up for a drink before they went clubbing.

He would then offer the landlords of these pubs an offer that they couldn't refuse. Regular cash payments and the supply of two doormen, who Scott paid for. The doormen would liaise with J.J. and Boz on the supply of what drugs were needed and to make sure the correct amount of cash was handed over to match the value of the drugs supplied. In this way, Scott could operate a very successful drug business and keep it well away from his clubs.

"Holly, you'd have to be really naive if you think none of our customers are using drugs. I've accepted this over the years, and as long as there is no dealing done in any of our clubs, what our customers get up to in their own time is a matter between the police and them. As you know, it is our door policy to search customers on a regular basis to make sure they are not bringing drugs, weapons, or any illicit booze into the clubs which would affect the safety of our operation and also the profitability of the clubs."

"So, is this why Jack came to Spain? Is this why he has formed a relationship with me and my family? He must think we supply the drugs."

"So, ask yourself why is he in Amsterdam, the drug capital of Europe, and not here in the U.K. investigating our family and our businesses?"

Holly just sat there, dumbfounded. She had no idea what to think. What was she going to say the next time she saw Jack? What if it was all true?

What she didn't know was at that moment in time, Jack was wondering if he would see Holly again as he was still tied to a chair with no food or water for the last two days.

Chapter Thirty-Five

Can Jack Escape?

Jack was really struggling. He had been sitting in this metal chair, hands and feet secured tightly with garden ties, and had now gone two days without any food or water.

The air was filled with the pungent smell of his urine, and he was now having difficulty in controlling his bowels.

Of course, he had tried to work himself loose. He had constantly rubbed the plastic ties that bound his ankles together. Unfortunately, the legs of the chair were round, and it was a lot of hard work to make any inroads into breaking free. He had also tried with his wrists behind his back, but all he could feel was the stickiness of the blood that was on his hands. He had no idea whether he had made any inroads to be able to snap the ties and break free before Big Chris returned. Was he ever going to come back? Surely, he wouldn't just let him starve to death.

To be true, it wasn't the lack of food that was the main problem, it was the raging thirst that he couldn't handle. His mouth was like old shoe leather, and he had given up ages ago shouting for help. He was totally screwed. What the hell could he do? He had heard the buzzing of his phone every time someone had rung, most probably Holly, but his phone was still firmly in his back pocket way out of reach.

It was the lights of an approaching car which must have given Jack some extra strength. He heard the car door being slammed and at the same time his feet broke free. Bloody miracle! But what to do now. He stood up and let the chair slip down. So he was free of the chair but still with his hands bound. He heard the door being unlocked, so he decided to sit back on the chair and feign being unconscious.

Big Chris entered the room and turned to switch all of the lights on. Jack saw his chance. He stood up. The clatter of the chair warned Big Chris. As he turned round, all he heard was the primal scream of a bent over raging animal. Big Chris was slow to react. Jack bent and headbutted Big Chris in the stomach. The big man fell to the floor. As he tried to get up, Jack used the freedom of his feet to kick Big Chris fiercely in the right side of his head. The speed of the big man trying to get up and the force of the kick rendered the big man unconscious, and he fell back.

As luck would have it, the flower man still had a set of commercial garden secateurs connected to his trouser belt. Straight away, Jack was able to rub the plastic ties up and down the edge of the sharp blade, and within a minute, his hands were free. Big Chris started making moaning sounds, so Jack quickly ran for the door to make good his escape before the big man regained consciousness.

He was in luck as the keys were still in Big Chris's car, so he made the decision to take the big man's car and drive it up the lane until he got to his own car. He got there really quickly and within minutes was on the main road to the airport. Thank God there was a bottle of water in his glove compartment. He drank it down in a huge gulp and tried to concentrate on his driving.

Now he knew where the drugs could be bought. He was astounded at the size of the operation. Rows and rows of flowers at the side of the road but going further in the field, the true nature of the business revealed itself with rows and rows of marijuana plants and fields of poppies. Although he had seen lots of chemical equipment in the room where he was kept captive, he didn't know if it was for the manufacture of Ecstasy tablets or cocaine, or both. All he knew it was a massive operation, and the transport required to get it into the U.K. was supplied by J.J., Boz, and an Augusta 109E helicopter.

How in the hell was he going to explain his movements over the last few days to Holly?

Chapter Thirty-Six

Jack reveals all to Mark

Jack was able to pass through customs at Schiphol Airport, so there was no need to stop off at Lydd. He was able to buy some painkillers for the pain in his hands and feet, and he made use of the medical bag on the Cessna to bandage up his right hand which was still bleeding through the cuts made by the plastic tees.

He didn't make the best of landings at Sywell Airport as it was just breaking dawn as he touched down really tired. Despite his tiredness, he got into the Lexus and headed off down to the hospital in London to bring Mark up to speed. Jack was hoping Mark might have remembered more of what happened when their father died.

It was just as he arrived at the Queen Elizabeth Hospital, that his mobile phone rang. It was Holly.

"Jack, Jack, I've been trying to reach you for days. I've been worried sick. What's happening? Why have you not returned my calls?" Holly was near to tears; she was that upset.

"Where are you now?" Jack asked, giving himself time to think what to tell Holly and also, what not to tell her.

"I'm at the Channel 4 T.V. studio to discuss my forthcoming television special. Where are you?"

"I'm going to be at Mark's bedside for a couple of hours. Can we meet up later?"

"I should be able to finish this meeting mid-morning. I'll walk across Lambeth Bridge and come straight to the hospital."

"See you later then, and don't worry."

Jack had no idea what to say to Holly when they finally met up. Perhaps it would be best to let her do most of the talking.

Mark was sitting up and looked 100 percent better than when Jack visited him last. The staff nurse allowed Jack to visit out of hours with the strict instructions not to stay too late and tire Mark out.

"Come on then, younger brother, spill the beans. What's been happening?"

Jack laughed at Mark's reference to the four minute age gap between the two of them.

He then proceeded to tell Mark everything about trying to track down the drug dealers who he thought had something to with their father's death. Commander James was convinced that a local nightclub owner had something to do with drug trade in London, but Jack argued that Scott Parker only dealt with soft drugs. The hard drugs that were beginning to flow into the capital was where the answer lay, and Jack was convinced J.J. had a lot to do with the trafficking of the drugs. He then went on to explain the complication of the Spain trip where he was supposed to find evidence against

Parker, but all he had done was fall in love with his daughter. Jack continued to tell Mark about the Amsterdam visits and the bandages around his wrists which told the tale of his escape.

"That's about all I can tell you now, Mark. Have you had any more flashbacks in your memories?"

"Well, you know Dad's Lexus. I keep dreaming a black one like Dad's is chasing me. Every time just as the car catches up with me in my dream, I wake up in a sweat."

Just then, Holly arrived. The atmosphere changed considerably as it was obvious Holly was ever so upset with Jack.

After introducing Holly to his brother, he said he would be back later, try and get some rest, he and Holly would be in the restaurant and would stay there until he woke up from his much needed sleep.

It was after they had both sat down with their coffees that Holly started to cry.

"Who are you, Jack? My dad says you are some sort of spy with MI5."

"What else has he been saying?"

"That you think our family are major drug dealers and are in some sort of turf war cumulating in the London club getting shot to pieces by an opposing gang. It all seems like something you would watch on Netflix."

Jack decided then to tell Holly some of the truth.

"Your dad's correct about my job. I obviously couldn't tell you what I do for a living as I've signed the Official Secrets Act. You must never, under any circumstances, repeat what I am about to tell you.

"I have discovered in a village near to Amsterdam where they are manufacturing drugs on a huge scale: heroin, Ecstasy tablets, marijuana, and possibly cocaine. Although I haven't seen any proof of that yet."

'Where does my father come into all this?"

"Your father might be one of the end users for his nightclubs and the events he is involved in."

"My father admits that his customers might be buying drugs before they enter into his clubs. He cannot be selling them, as all of his doormen have strict instructions to search customers who might have drugs on them, knives or illegal booze as well. He does everything he can to keep drugs out of his clubs."

"I accept that, Holly, and we have no evidence to prove otherwise. Obviously, our main aim is to find the source of the drugs supply and shut it down with harsh penalties in prison for those involved in the drug trade. You must know how serious these criminals are when they can go into your dad's club and completely wreck it with repeating rifles and one or two light submachine guns. The police found over 1000 shells when they searched the club after the raid but, as far as I'm aware, they are no nearer to find out who the gang is and, more importantly, who is the gang's leader."

"Well, Jack, I have come here today to tell you I am supporting my dad 100 percent, and until this matter is all cleared up, I don't think we should see each other."

With that, Holly stood up, turned around, and walked out of the hospital restaurant.

Chapter Thirty-Seven

Bruno has a plan

Bruno Grigoryan was having a bad day. Frustrated at not finding Scott Parker or any of his family at The Rooftop Gardens, he now had to deal with the matter of one of his girls attempting to go back to Albania.

"Come in." Bruno sat up in his office chair and placed his hand in his right-hand office drawer. The Walther PK would slide into his hand immediately if things were to turn nasty.

The girl entered the room. Bruno pointed at the chair on the other side of his desk and motioned for her to sit down.

"Lisa, isn't it?" The girl nodded.

"I hear that you are that unhappy here, Lisa, and you have tried to leave us." The girl remained silent.

"Well, Lisa, I have decided that I will let you go home. What do you think to that?"

Lisa sat up straight, smiled at Bruno. and couldn't believe her ears.

"Thank you, thank you!"

"There is the small matter of your bill. I see here you have been with us for nearly six months now."

Bruno pretended he was reading the figures from a sheet of paper he had on his desk.

"Well, that's 200 pounds a week for accommodation, a further 100 pounds a week for your meals and drinks so, with interest, we are talking nearly 10,000 pounds owed. Have you got that sort of money, Lisa?"

The girl just sobbed and shook her head.

"Well, you're going to have to keep on working for me until you pay your debts, do you understand?" Lisa just nodded and slumped back into her chair.

"Do you remember Charleen, the young Austrian girl who had an unfortunate accident a while back, and her face was so badly injured she was unable to work? Apparently, she was trying to get back home when the accident happened. Now, we wouldn't want that to happen to you, Lisa, would we?"

Bruno pressed a button underneath his desktop, the office door opened and Grigor, Bruno's right-hand man, entered.

"Grigor, take Lisa back to her room now and, whilst you're there, will you give her just a small reminder of what will happen if she tries to go home without paying her debts before she goes?"

Grigor's eyes brightened up. "Sure thing, boss."

"Make sure you shut all the doors as we don't want to wake any of the other girls in their afternoon naps; we have a busy night ahead of us."

Bruno now turned his thoughts to Scott Parker who, he was sure, was responsible for his cousin Navik's death and disappearance.

Raiding Parker's club was a knee jerk reaction which he regretted. A simple phone call to the club the day after the raid had told him Mr. Parker wasn't available to come to the phone as he and his wife were on holiday in Thailand. He was going to have to be a little bit more thoughtful about how to deal with him when he returned. The raid on the club had attracted too many press headlines, and now the Metropolitan police were all over it. He would have to lie low and bide his time. Perhaps if Scott Parker's daughter, Holly, were persuaded to join his group of girls then maybe Parker would come to him, and Bruno wouldn't have the bother of searching him out.

Chapter Thirty-Eight

Holly's in Danger

Jack didn't know what to do. At the last briefing, Commander James had ordered 24-hour surveillance on the Parker family and no mention at all about his own son. *Why would he?* thought Jack. Jack was the only one who knew about the activities of J.J. and his sidekick Boz and, obviously, Commander James thought his only son could do no wrong even though he was connected to the Parker family through his schooldays friendship with Scott's son, John.

So here he was, stuck in the middle of Rutland taking turns doing eight-hour shift work to make sure Scott Parker was followed wherever he went.

His partner, Iain, a long-term MI5 agent well-experienced in this type of work put down his binoculars and said, "Well, Jack, if you want my opinion, Parker knows he's under surveillance. He has been watched now for just over a week and nothing. I thought he had a legitimate business to run. Who's supervising the repairs to his London club? Who's running his other clubs? Surely, he cannot be doing it all on the end of a phone."

They were parked in a lay-by which gave them a clear view of the Parkers' residence. A long gravel driveway leading to a six bedroom house complete with tennis court completed the image a successful businessman can afford. There had been nothing during their shift, no movement whatsoever.

It was approaching midnight, the end of their shift, and Jack was looking forward to going back to their hotel, write up his daily report, and getting some well-earned rest.

The headlights of another car approaching them suddenly turned into the driveway. The car stopped at the front door of the house, and Holly got out.

"That's Parker's Jaguar, and that's his daughter, Holly," Jack informed his partner. "Wait a minute, what the hell's happening!"

Jack grabbed the binoculars. Two men emerged from the shadows of the front of the house. One rushed forward to open the back door of the car, whilst the bigger man of the two grabbed Holly from behind, covered her mouth with one hand, and with the other, lifted her up and bundled her into the back seat of her car. In a matter of seconds, the car was driving out of the driveway, and with the sound of tyres screeching, they drove out of the driveway, turned right, and accelerated past the surveillance car.

"Quick, for Christ's sake, they're getting away!"

Iain started up the car and very quickly made a three point turn to give chase.

They could not see any tell-tale rear red lights of Holly's Jaguar, so they just assumed the car had

192

gone straight on. They were now doing over 100 miles an hour, and they could still not see anything.

Grigor just smiled as, through his rear mirror, he could see the surveillance car shoot past the first turn that Grigor had made. They had quickly switched cars. After transferring a still struggling Holly to their own car, they quite sedately drove off so as not to attract any attention from nosey neighbours. Keeping well within all the speed limits, they made their way back to London where they knew Bruno would be waiting up to welcome their new guest.

Chapter Thirty-Nine

Scott Receives a Call

It was two o'clock in the morning when Scott's personal phone buzzed at the side of his bed. He quickly answered it so as not to awaken Harriet.

"Hello," Scott sat up in his bed with his phone to his ear.

"Mr. Parker, Mr. Scott Parker."

"Yes, this is Scott Parker, and who the hell are you calling me at this time of the night, and how in the hell did you get my number?"

Scott spoke as he swiftly got out of bed and went into the en-suite bathroom to continue the call.

"My name is Bruno Grigoryan. You might have met my cousin, Navik, yes?"

"I've never heard of you or your brother. Now what in the hell do you want?"

"To answer your earlier question, I obtained your mobile number from your daughter, Holly."

"Have you got my daughter? I'll bloody kill you if you have harmed her in any way."

"Yes, I have got her in a manner of speaking. I went to your club to meet up with you but, unfortunately, you were on holiday. Thailand, I believe, so I left behind my calling card. Did you appreciate it?" Bruno's metallic laughter reverberated down the mobile phone.

"What do you want?!" screamed Scott into the phone. Harriet was now at his shoulder fully awake.

"I want to meet up, Mr. Parker, and as I've already tried to come to you, I would appreciate it if, this time, you could come to me. Possibly so I could return your daughter to you."

"When and where? I want my daughter back as soon as possible," Scott was on the verge of totally losing it.

"Let's be adult about this. How about we meet today at your favourite restaurant, The Ivy in London, say one o'clock. I'll let you make the booking." With that, he rang off.

Scott arrived early at The Ivy, making sure the maître d' allocated his favourite table by the window so Scott could see the whole restaurant, and also his table would be the first for anyone entering the restaurant.

Scott didn't know what to expect as he looked up and down waiting for the new arrival. He had to look twice at the man who entered the restaurant exactly at one o'clock. Bruno was dressed immaculately. A black, superbly cut two-piece suit, shoes so highly polished you could see your face in them, a crisp white shirt, no tie, as was the fashion, and a sharp haircut any Premiership footballer would be proud of.

Bruno held out his hand as he approached Scott, which was ignored.

"Sit down, and tell me where my daughter is."

"She is close by, totally unhurt and will join us after we have finished talking business."

"Me do business with you? You must be joking," Scott was on the point of walking out.

"Listen, Mister Parker, I can understand your actions killing two of my cousins in Spain. They were too bull headed in their business dealings. I was only too happy to help my cousin Navik when he sought revenge but, can't you see, from a business point of view, these killings are getting us nowhere. I have inherited Navik's heroin business which, to be frank, I know nothing about. I would much rather stick to what I know best. I look to you to help me sort out some sort of arrangement where you can buy my heroin and make sure it is distributed the same way as your other drugs."

Scott sat back in his chair, waived away the waiter as he approached the table, and replied, "I've never dealt in heroin as I know I will have to deal with the fallout of customers killing themselves, which will bring police involvement investigating me. I've been lucky as I haven't had that up until now."

"Mister Parker, I want us to be business partners. I want you to be the main distributer for my goods, and I want to give you your daughter back. I have come up with a solution that I hope you will agree to. What about you sell my heroin on say a Tuesday or a Wednesday, one of the quieter nights? Regular customers will know where and when to get their supply, and there won't be any problems on your busy weekend nights where you can concentrate on selling your soft drugs. What do you think? Like I said, I don't want a war which will do neither of us any good. As an act of good faith, I will leave now, and your daughter will be here in a few minutes. Please take a couple of days and think about what I have said. I don't want any more deaths, and I can guarantee, if you agree to the new deal, your daughter will always be safe. Unfortunately, if you decide that is the road you want to go down, I have to tell you I have twice the men and twice the guns, so it is a war you will not win."

With that, Bruno got up and left. Scott was left there deep in thought which was broken by the hysterical sobbing of his daughter rushing into his arms.

"Thank God you are safe darling, are you alright? Did they hurt you?"

"I'm fine, Dad, they didn't touch me. I was just so scared. Why did they kidnap me? Who are these men, what do they do?"

"They are drug dealers who want me to go in business with them. Don't worry, darling, you're safe now and your safety, and that of our family, will be my first priority."

Scott held his daughter tighter as he realised he was between a rock and a hard place. He had to deal in heroin or he had to start a war, neither of which he wanted to do.

He knew his decision had to be to go into business with Bruno to guarantee his family's safety. He tried to tell himself perhaps the sale of heroin mid-week wouldn't be that much. In his heart, he knew he was kidding himself.

The stakes were now too high for him to do anything else.

Chapter Forty

Jack gets permission

Jack entered the MI5 building feeling nervous and very unsure of himself. Ever since he had passed the final test, the kindly doorman, Bob, always spoke to Jack, asked how his brother was, and, this morning, wished him well with his meeting later on with Commander James. Was there nothing in the building Bob didn't know about? Bob must have noticed how wound up Jack was to wish him well.

Jack went to the toilet to check his appearance and to take a few deep breaths. He was about to tell Commander James about how he had discovered Big Chris and his drug business. Jack needed his boss's permission to contact the drug Interpol office in Brussels to plan a raid and, hopefully, catch whoever was delivering the drugs to the U.K. No way could Jack tell his boss how he came to know about the exact time of the deliveries as that would entail Jack blowing the whistle on J.J. and Boz. Commander James had already made his position on both his son and his sidekick's innocence, so Jack decided not to tell him all of the details he had planned for the raid.

"Come in," Commander James had his nose in some paperwork as he motioned Jack to take a seat. It was several minutes before he spoke again. "At last, young Jack, you have some news about how all the drugs in the U.K. are sourced."

"A piece of luck really, sir. I was in Amsterdam recently on a weekend's leave when I got talking to the proprietor of a cafe. I ended up just asking where could I buy a substantial amount of drugs to import into the U.K., and he gave me the details of a relative of his, a guy known as Big Chris, who was responsible for suppling marijuana and Ecstasy tablets to most of the outlets in the city.

"I made two visits to Big Chris, one in the daytime where he told me his business was commercially growing flowers. This checked out as on the drive to his office, I passed row upon row of greenhouses growing flowers. The second clandestine visit I made in the early hours of the morning. The first two rows of greenhouses did indeed grow flowers, but the rows after that grew marijuana plants and then rows and rows of poppy fields."

"You've done well, Jack, anything else?"

"I also managed to break into a building where it turned out to be the place where the chemists made the Ecstasy tablets and possibly cocaine."

"How do you know when there are any deliveries made? Do they transport the drugs back to the U.K. by boat, aeroplane, or just by trucks?"

"That's why I need your permission to contact Interpol, set up a joint operation and stakeout and be there when the deliveries are being made. We can

200

then, hopefully, capture the drug gangs in one fell swoop."

"Our contact at Interpol in their office in Brussels is their Executive Director for Police Services Alan Griffiths. I'll e-mail him and ask for his help. Hopefully, he'll provide you with a S.W.A.T. team. Where will you be based?" asked Commander James.

"I stayed at the Hilton in Amsterdam. It's as good as any to base ourselves, as I will have at least two hours' notice from my intel before the drug transaction is made. Plenty of time to get to the location and set up good sniper positions in case things go pear shape, and they don't do the sensible thing and give themselves up."

"Any idea of their strength of armament?"

"Well, Big Chris, I know for sure is armed. I have no doubt they will have small arms, but we must be prepared to go in with tear gas and flash grenades if they carry AK47 submachine guns and the like. The ideal situation is to capture the main dealers alive so we can take them back to the U.K. and, hopefully, get some valuable intel from them."

"Well, good luck. Let me know if there is anything I can get for you to help you with your mission."

Jack left his boss's office with mixed emotions. Here he was planning an operation where one of the criminals he was planning to capture was a high ranking officer in MI5's son! A very delicate situation indeed.

Jack got the train home where he was pleasantly surprised when Susan picked him up from the station accompanied with Mark who seemed to be getting better day by day.

It was after dinner that Jack asked Mark if he fancied a walk around their garden so they could have a chat and, perhaps, Mark would be able to give Jack some advice. Jack knew his operational skills, along with the help of Interpol, would go a long way to the success of the mission. It was the probability that Jack, using his Glock 17 pistol, might have to shoot at their adversaries and, if worse came to worse, Jack might have to kill someone. Was he capable of taking another man's life? He had no idea. He decided against telling Mark about his worries. Mark's memory was improving slightly but not enough to help Jack identify their father's killers and the reason behind what happened to them both.

J.J. and Boz were driving over to Sywell to pick up the helicopter after its 50 hour service. J.J. had had the usual instructions when to fly over to Haarlem to drop off the newly delivered cardboard box containing the cash, and he already had the five grand in his pocket. As the delivery wasn't going to take place for a couple of days, J.J. decided he and Boz needed a cracking night out. After flying back to his hangar, he and Boz rode the B.M.W. motorbike down to London to spend the night at one of J.J.'s favourite 'Gay' clubs. The five grand was quickly spent on Cristal Champagne, which, along with copious amounts of cocaine, soon had J.J. and Boz spiralling into another world.

The next day when J.J, finally came round about midday, he checked his phone. There was another message from the man with the electronic voice. He must have left it when J.J. was partying at the club. Maybe because it was in a basement the signal was no good. It just came across as a garbled message saying something about Haarlem. J.J. was suffering the worst hangover he had ever endured, and he just thought the man with the electronic voice was firming up the details for that night's delivery. He wasn't to know it was Commander James, who after receiving Jack's plan to stop the raid, was sending a message to his son to cancel the delivery. J.J. took off that night at his normal time of 2 am heading for disaster.

Chapter Forty-One

Jack plans the Raid

Jack was sitting at his desk in the Hilton Hotel at Schiphol Airport Amsterdam writing a report so he could bring the S.W.A.T. officer up to date. The hotel phone by his bedside rang, and the receptionist informed Jack there was a Charlie McIntosh waiting downstairs in the hotel's conference room for their one o'clock meeting.

Jack was pleasantly surprised when, whilst shaking the officers hand, discovered Charlie was a woman.

"Don't look so surprised. I have the experience and the knowledge to help you with your mission." Charlie laughed at Jack's reaction. They shook hands and straight away got to work.

Using a white board, Jack drew out a rough plan of the dirt track they would go down, the area where the greenhouses started, the main reception area where, presumably, Big Chris was based, and finally, the last building where the chemists worked and produced the Ecstasy tablets.

Pointing at this last building, Jack explained, "This is where the Augusta 109E helicopter landed and, very swiftly, was able to transfer cash for the drugs. I assume it was all heroin as the Ecstasy tablets and marijuana drugs are kept back for local use within Amsterdam."

"Do you think if we just drive up and introduce ourselves they will let us arrest them?" asked Charlie.

Jack thought back to the two days of hell Big Chris had succumbed him to and shook his head.

"To these people, the drugs are everything. They only tolerate each other because it suits their business plan. I get the impression once someone is of no longer of any use to them, they will soon be dealt with."

"Any idea how many on either side of the delivery we will be dealing with?"

"Well, I'm assuming there will only be two in the helicopter, the pilot and an ex-army sharpshooter. They have delivered before and, as everything went well, they'll only be carrying small arms. The same, hopefully, with the gang who will be there waiting for the delivery of cash. Their main concern will be to hand over the heroin and for everything to go off smoothly like before. So, in the answer to your question, I shouldn't think more than six in total."

"I think you and I should approach from the front. You've met this guy Big Chris before, and maybe, just maybe, he'll see the sense of just giving up and be prepared to do some jail time instead of getting involved in a heavy duty fire fight."

As Charlie was explaining this tactic, Jack was slowly shaking his head. "That puts you and me in a very dangerous position."

"Because of that, let's put two of our guys positioned behind the building where Big Chris is, both ready to act as soon as anything kicks off. Also we can put two men on the opposite side of the dirt track to protect us, ready to eliminate Big Chris and his back-up."

Charlie drew the positions on the whiteboard, and they both stood back and looked at the set up.

"How long do you think we'll have to stay here at the hotel and wait for the next delivery?"

"I have a tracker on the helicopter, so as soon as it takes off, never in daylight, then we have an hour and a half to get us and our equipment in position. I suggest we let it land and begin the transfer before we make our move. It's nearly a month since the last flight, so I am assuming if they are scheduled for monthly deliveries, it could happen any day now."

Charlie responded by informing Jack that she would have her team at the hotel before sundown, and the arms and equipment would be in the minibus they would be using. After thoroughly briefing her team, to save time, they would change into their body armour. To protect their arms and legs, they would wear bullet-proof Kevlar, and to protect the more vital parts of their bodies, i.e. their heads and their torsos, they would wear clothing that was made of a mix of Kevlar and ceramic material ensuring no penetration from the bullets of small arms and, hopefully, rifle fire.

Jack and the team spent the next two days going over different scenarios if things were to go pear shaped and, with Charlie's input, he was sure he had the mission covered. A clean arrest and no body bags would be the ideal solution.

Every night at 6 pm, his thoughts went to calling Holly on his mobile. His heart ached for the girl, and he was gutted that her dad had spilled the beans. He would have to tell her everything if there was to be any hope for a future together, and to be honest, he didn't see much hope of that happening.

Overnight, the team sat waiting for the magic hour of 2 am, the time J.J. took off on his last delivery. Jack hoped it would be the same. It was two nights later when the tension was broken at 2 am when the alarm sound for the tracker went off on Jack's phone. The helicopter was on its way.

Immediately, everyone in the team gathered up their equipment and made their way out of the hotel into the waiting mini-bus and with a screech of tyres, were on their way to the target.

Chapter Forty-Two

All Hell Breaks Loose

An hour after they had left the hotel, the mini-bus was unloaded and hid in the same place Jack had left his car on his previous second visit at night.

The mile walk to their objective was done in complete silence after a quick radio check to make sure that they could all communicate with each other. They stopped at their pre-organised places a little bit further back in the darkness, so they couldn't be seen or heard by the waiting three-man loading team.

There was movement in the building leading to the three figures making six to be potentially dealt with.

Jack couldn't believe what he was seeing. Scott Parker was one of the men, Big Chris the other and making up this new business consortium was what looked like one of the Grigoryan family that Jack hadn't had the privilege of meeting yet. Whatever happened to Scott Parker's pledge not to deal in hard core drugs?

The back officers guarding Jack and Charlie's rear position also had a strong battery searchlight which was planned to be switched on to illuminate the target area and also used to make sure everyone involved in the drugs transaction was aware they were caught in the act and, if they had any sense, would just hold up their hands and surrender. If no surrender was likely and the drugs gang started shooting first, Jack was prepared to hit them with rifle-launched flash grenades and canisters of tear gas.

Jack and Charlie were in position with two officers a little way to the rear watching their back. The remaining two officers were positioned to the rear of the chemical building to cut off any possible retreat.

The men were just standing around chatting when all heads turned at the distant sound of the approaching helicopter.

Jack and Charlie ducked as the Augusta approached into wind with the strong landing light illuminating their position for a couple of seconds.

The helicopter turned at the last minute to make a perfect landing just beyond the group of men. They patiently waited until the rotors stopped spinning and the jet engine was turned off. After the loud noise of the helicopter, the silence was eerie until Big Chris took command and started barking orders.

J.J. and Boz descended from the machine carrying two large holdalls obviously containing the large amount of cash required to buy the prepared load of heroin.

It was after Big Chris had checked the contents of the two holdalls, and J.J. had checked the purity of the heroin, that both teams started to carry out the tasks for the evening. It was at this point that Jack stood, the searchlight was switched on, and using a police megaphone, he shouted at the groups.

"Stop, you are all under arrest. Lay down your arms or we will be forced to open fire."

All of the gang looked in the direction of the voice but because of the power of the searchlight, they couldn't make out anything.

Big Chris was the first to react. Moving very quickly for a man of his size, he dashed through the front door of the chemical building only to emerge holding an AK47 machine gun and promptly started to spray 300 rounds a minute in the general direction of the searchlight. Big Chris was also the first casualty. He was still trying to run towards Jack and Charlie, so one of the back-up officers opened fire. Big Chris finally stopped and, with look of complete puzzlement on his face, looked down at the gaping hole in his chest. He dropped his machine gun and slowly toppled over with a red mist of gushing blood spraying all over his prostrate body.

This signalled for all hell to let loose. J.J. immediately turned and re-entered the Augusta to start up the engine. Boz, realising what his boss was trying to do, knelt and gave covering fire into an area where he could still not distinguish any targets. The three guys who were doing the loading at the side of the helicopter now ran into the side of the track away from the light of the searchlight. The last one of the loaders turned to return fire. He should have continued his run into the darkness but was knocked back at least 10 metres as a shot from Charlie's Armalite rifle nearly cut him in two. Bruno was the next to be hit. His pistol was like a peashooter compared to the firepower he was facing, and after being hit in the shoulder, he threw his pistol onto the ground and raised his good arm in surrender.

Scott took advantage of the mayhem to run and take cover in the chemical building.

Charlie then made a really brave move breaking cover to fire a rifle grenade into the front door of the building only to take a hit from one of the loader's rifles. She tried to walk back to her previous position but only managed to fall to the ground. Under covering fire, Jack managed to drag her back into the safety of the darkness. Meanwhile, the noise of the helicopter starting up filled the air. Boz was now aiming at the back-up officers behind Jack and Charlie. With a loud grunt of pain, it was clear one of the officers had been hit. Jack stood up and threw a tear gas canister towards the front of the building.

This brought an immediate result. Scott Parker emerged from the building coughing and spluttering. Holding his arms aloft, he quickly lay down beside Bruno in an act of complete surrender. The two officers at the rear of the building had done a great job. On hearing the rifle grenade going off, they made their way around the side of the building only to come up behind the two remaining loaders who stood to attention with arms raised, were quickly handcuffed, and told to kneel down. This only left Boz who was still loyally protecting his boss. J.J. screamed at him to climb on board as the helicopter was ready to take off. Boz managed to put one foot on the skid on the passenger side and was just about to open the door to safety but was struck by a rifle bullet in the back of his neck. J.J. lifted the collective lever of the helicopter controls to facilitate a really fast take off. The machine rose like a champagne cork coming out of its bottle. If Boz's arm weren't covered in blood, perhaps he could have held on and escaped along with J.J. The pilot could only concentrate on his flying. He only heard the scream of Boz as he finally had to let go. Jack looked up to see the body of Boz twirling around and around until he heard the thud of the body hitting the ground above the sound of the departing helicopter.

Whilst the officers handcuffed Bruno and Scott, Jack checked on Charlie. She had been knocked out with a rifle shot to the head, but due to the Kevlar and ceramic helmet, she quickly came round with no more than a headache. Jack assessed the damage to the drugs gang. Three dead and one with a shoulder bullet wound. One escapee. Charlie was OK, but one of the back-up officers had taken a hit in his upper arm which had penetrated, but he was still able to walk. Jack decided to come back in the morning to clear away the carnage and collect the bodies.

212

Because of all the action, nobody had noticed the rifle grenade had caused a fire starting in the chemical building. Jack ordered everyone to retreat back to the mini-bus. They were halfway back when there was an enormous explosion. Jack looked back to witness an enormous tower of flames erupting into the sky only to land, and set alight, the first row of greenhouses. Jack thought it was ironic that one part of the drug-producing business was about to destroy the poppies and the marijuana. He smiled to himself as he had no intention to call any fire brigade assistance to help put out the spreading flames.

Only when he was back at the mini-bus did he realise one thing: throughout the whole of the action, he hadn't fired his gun. It was still in its holster.

J.J. was still shaking when he brought the Augusta to a hover over his hanger waiting for the roof to open. His rotor blades narrowly missed sending the helicopter into a million bits, but J.J. managed to regain control just in time. A few minutes later, the skids settled on the ground, and James waited for the rotors to slow down and eventually stop. He pressed the remote for the roof to close and got out of the helicopter. He switched on the L.E.D. lights then started to inspect it for bullet holes. He was sure it had taken a few hits. He grimaced as he saw Boz's blood smeared over the passenger skid. He was still inspecting it when a voice behind him startled him and caused him to swiftly turn around. He froze and, for once, was completely speechless.

Chapter Forty-Three

Jack reports back

After only a couple of hours' sleep, both Charlie and Jack made out a written report of the previous night's mission. Her team had taken Scott Parker and the two surviving loaders straight to prison and Bruno Grigoryan to the prison hospital to get the bullet removed from his shoulder. Two officers were sent to the scene of the previous night's action only to report back that all three bodies had been burned to a crisp in the ensuing fire that had completely destroyed the chemical building, the offices, and all of the greenhouses. All that was left was row upon row of burnt out shells. *A brilliant result*, thought Jack.

So, when he telephoned Commander James to give him a verbal report on the successful mission, his boss, strangely subdued, insisted on hearing it in person and could Jack get a flight back as soon as possible. He would have a driver pick him up at Heathrow and bring Jack to his house on the southeast coast instead of the London office. Jack thought this a bit strange. Had his boss found out about his son's nocturnal activities?

Jack couldn't sleep that night and was really pleased when his brother, Mark, answered his mobile. Jack went through the details of the mission with Mark who congratulated his brother on a successful result. Jack then went on to tell Mark about his worries about Holly. He had put her dad into prison where he was looking at several years' jail time. What was that going to do their relationship?

"Surely, if the girl didn't know about the drugs side of her father's business, she'll come round to your way of thinking. What were you supposed to do when her father suddenly appeared in the middle of an operation?"

Jack didn't have much confidence in Mark's summing up of the situation. Holly's dad would be looking at several years' hard time, and Jack didn't think for a minute he and Holly would be able to survive that.

Mark went on to tell Jack that he had remembered how their father had died. He explained about the drug buy that went wrong, the ensuing car chase, and how their dad's warning shout had saved Mark's life.

"My memory's getting better all the time. Perhaps when you've finished your debrief tomorrow, we can meet up in town to go through lots of things that have started to come clear."

Jack switched his mobile phone to off. It was brilliant that Mark was getting his memory back. Would there be a time when they would be working together? Jack wasn't too sure. Although the operation had turned out alright, J.J. had still escaped and, if Jack was honest with himself, it was Charlie who was the real hero of the night. With his adrenalin still buzzing from the previous night's action, Jack knew he wouldn't get a good night's rest. Tossing and turning, it was after four o'clock when he finally fell asleep.

Jack caught the first flight from Amsterdam to Heathrow the next morning. The driver was a big sort of gruff fellow who didn't speak, which suited Jack as it gave him time to think. It was when the driver turned the Mercedes into the gravel driveway of the impressive Georgian building that Jack, for some reason, started to feel a bit apprehensive.

Why did Commander James want to have the debrief at his home? He should be elated at the result of the mission but for some reason, he felt things weren't quite right. Perhaps his boss would give him his answers.

Jack had tried to phone Mark that morning to tell him he wasn't, in fact, in London for the debrief but at his boss's house. There was no answer, so Jack had just left a message telling Mark he couldn't meet up with him in London as they had planned, as he would be at the south coast most of the day, but he would be at home in Middleton in the evening, and he was looking forward to catching up.

The driver drove away which left Jack at the front door ringing the bell. While he was waiting, he looked around at the magnificent grounds and the fabulous view overlooking the sea. His boss was obviously a very wealthy man to be able to live in such splendour. Perhaps it was old money, and he had inherited it all.

Just then, the door opened. It was J.J., and he was holding a Glock G19 handgun pointing directly at Jack's stomach.

Chapter Forty-Four

The Final Showdown

Jack was still in a state of shock walking into the large hall of the house with J.J. prodding him in the back occasionally with his pistol to make sure he was reminded not to try and make his escape.

They entered a large library room to be met by Commander James with his back to the roaring fire, smoking his pipe, as though there was nothing amiss.

"Ah, young Stevens, here you are. I hope you had a pleasant flight from Amsterdam after your exertions of the previous night."

"What the hell is going on? You obviously know, by now, of your son's involvement in the delivery of large amounts of heroin into the U.K."

"Yes, a stroke of genius what! When James arrived home rather late, we had the first conversation we've had for months. For him to discover it was me who masterminded a great deal of the heroin being brought into the UK, he was quite impressed, and I believe it was you, James, that said we would make a great partnership." With that, J.J. nodded his head in approval.

"When I discovered that my only son had bought himself a helicopter, I decided that he would be my new method of transport. I had had two previous shipments picked up by the immigration police who had been on the lookout for illegals coming into the country only to stop and search my boats and, lucky for them, find two million pounds' worth of heroin. I had to electronically disguise my voice when I offered my son the delivery job as, at the time, I didn't want him to be aware of my business dealings. I knew a sum of 5000 pounds per delivery would tempt him and also ensure his silence. It was all going perfectly well until you got lucky finding out where he kept his machine. Even for you, two and two made four, so it must have been a simple job of following the helicopter whenever it took off."

Jack was getting really pissed off with the man's arrogance.

"So, this is why you wanted me to assassinate Scott Parker, to open up an inroad into his clubs and events to sell heroin. Why do you need to? You obviously don't need the money."

"That's where you're wrong, young man. I'm a commander in Her Majesty's Secret Service on a mere pittance compared to a commander in the police force. They get paid three times what I earn. I have this house and its grounds to upkeep and, also, my villa in the South of France. I wouldn't have this lifestyle if I just tried to live on my basic salary. Besides, I do rather like the excitement of it all. Don't you?"

"Your exciting lifestyle killed three people in order for you to continue importing drugs that will undoubtedly kill hundreds more."

"Well, you know what they say. You can lead a horse to water."

With that, Commander James put his hand behind his back and revealed the presence of his Walther PPK pistol.

Shit, thought Jack. *I've got all this knowledge of what kind of gun is which, and here I am facing a gun made famous by James Bond.*

Jack was totally shocked when the gun was raised in his direction only for it to turn sideways and fire a 9 millimetre bullet into the heart of J.J.'s body. Before the commander could alter his aim to fire again, the onrush of Jack's body felled the commander in a perfect rugby tackle. Jack had time to kick the Walther PPK away and swiftly remove his own Glock 19 pistol.

"Don't move an inch, or I will blow your head to bits. What in the hell are you doing? You've just killed your only son."

"Well, Jack, I have a sea plane landing just off the seashore in 30 minutes who will fly me to a destination I have had ready for a few years now just in case my cover was eventually blown. The last thing I needed to do was to eliminate all of the loose ends and, unfortunately, you and James know too much." The commander made a move to pick up his pistol.

"What do you think you're doing? Stay perfectly still, or I will shoot you."

"You see, young Jack, that's where you are wrong. I don't think you will shoot me in cold-blood. You just simply haven't got the guts to kill another human being."

With that, he bent down, picked up his pistol, stood up, and raised his arm to take aim.

Jack just stood there. He also raised his arm to point his gun. It was just like an old fashioned duel.

There was another loud bang that filled the room as a gun went off sending a deadly 9 millimetre bullet directly to its target. There was the sound of a body falling to the floor.

Jack couldn't believe he was still alive as he opened his eyes, turned his body, only to see his brother, Mark, standing in the doorway, gun still raised, smoke still pouring from the barrel.

"Mark! Thank God you're here."

"Good job, bro, that one of us has no problem being an assassin."

Both brothers walked towards each other, and Jack's thankful handshake turned into an embrace. Neither brother could think of anything to say.

It was later when they were waiting for the local police to come and take charge of what effectively was a crime scene, that Jack asked Mark what made him decide to come down to the south coast that day.

"You know how I've got my memory back? I went on the computer to read about our father and grandfather's experiences acting on behalf of the Directive. It suddenly twigged that every mission had to be authorised by four high ranking officers including a member of the Royal Family. I went with our father to the Military Club in London to a meeting where the committee of the Directive had decided they had to take strong action against whoever was bringing vast amounts of drugs into the U.K. Normally, the Directive was only used in a time of war but all four men, including the royal, agreed that this was, indeed, a war. A war on drugs.

"After investigating, it was up to our father's discretion to assassinate the perpetrators.

"Every meeting over the years had been held with four men discussing cases that could be handled outside the usual course of law. Jack, did you ever attend such a meeting?"

"No," replied Jack. "All of my meetings were with Commander James and him alone, and I've never even been to the Military Club."

"So, you see, Jack, the man was just getting you trained up to become his personal hitman to further his drug empire."

"If it had been decided that I had to make a decision to kill someone, apart from it being completely illegal, it would have shown straight away my complete reluctance to do such a thing. Guess I'm just not cut for MI5. I think I'll just hand in my resignation and go back to flying. I'm so glad you decided to come down, Mark. I would be floating in the sea feeding the fishes if you hadn't."

A couple of days later, Jack and Charlie attended the hearing at the Old Bailey where Scott Parker was denied bail. His wife, Harriet, just started to sob, and Holly never looked over at Jack. Not once that day did their eyes meet.

Jack was pleased bail had been denied as it gave Charlie and him all the time they needed to interview Scott in his cell at Gartree, a category B prison in Market Harborough, near to where Jack lived.

"Right, Scott, this is the second time we have interviewed you and, for the benefit of the tape, those in attendance are yourself, Scott Parker; myself, Jack Stevens; and Interpol Drug Officer, Charlie McIntosh.

"In our first interview, you denied any knowledge of the deaths of two drug dealers in Spain even though you had a military sharpshooter, Michael Bosnic, known as 'Boz', on your payroll who was killed in the shootout attempting to escape. I don't think for one minute you didn't have anything to do with it.

"Never mind all of this. We have successfully destroyed a huge drug operation where the main players have been killed. All we need from you now is the connection you have in Thailand for the import of your cocaine."

"What would there be in it for me if I was to disclose my contacts?" admitted Scott.

"Scott, you're looking at 8-10 years' hard time. If you co-operate, we can look at reducing the sentence and move you into an open prison. We accept you went into the drugs business only at Ecstasy and cocaine level but stupidly soon graduated to the harder drugs. Why did you do that?"

"They had captured my daughter and threatened to do it again if I didn't allow them to use my supply lines for their product. I was stuck between a rock and a hard place. In the end, I had no choice."

The trial three weeks later didn't last long, as Scott, in the end, decided to plead guilty, and he received a sentence of five years.

Chapter Forty-Five

The Epilogue

Jack never saw Holly again. He made no attempt to contact her and no matter how many times he checked his phone, there was no voice mail from her.

It was several years later when Mark and he were standing in the queue at Harrods. Jack was holding hands with his five-year-old daughter, Penelope, and Mark was standing next to them holding the hand of his very impatient son, Michael.

All four were waiting to see Father Christmas.

Jack had got to know Charlie with the work they both had to do clearing up all the details to be sent to the prosecution service for the trial of Scott Parker. Parker was sentenced to five years' imprisonment, but if he behaved himself, he would be out in three.

It came as quite a surprise to both Charlie and Jack when they fell in love and nine months after being married, came the blessed addition of baby Penelope.

They had just about reached the front of the queue when Mark prodded Jack.

"Jack, isn't that Holly and her family walking into the balcony restaurant?"

Jack looked over and immediately recognised the beautiful Holly. Scott's son, John, was there.

Jack had heard through the grapevine that John now ran the drug-free business with Scott and Harriet now retired. The T.V. special for Holly was never commissioned. Funny how being the daughter of a drug king can decimate one's career. Jack didn't even think she was gigging which was a sad waste.

Jack was pleased the family had sorted themselves out. Scott Parker had turned queen's evidence and had received a lighter sentence and eventually served three years in an open prison.

Jack had left the Secret Service, joined the RAF and was now flying with the Red Arrows leaving the Secret Service work to his wife, Charlie, and his twin brother, Mark.

Jack took one last look at the family as they sat for lunch. He often wondered how it all would have ended if he hadn't been such a reluctant assassin.

Printed in Poland
by Amazon Fulfillment
Poland Sp. z o.o., Wrocław

62636325R00134